SECRETS OF
THE ITALIAN
GARDENER

SECRETS OF
THE ITALIAN
GARDENER

ANDREW CROFTS

RedDoor

Published by RedDoor
www.reddoorpublishing.com

ISBN 978-1-910453-38-4

Cover design: Elliot Thomson at novakcollective.com
Typesetting: www.typesetter.org.uk
Print managed by Jellyfish Solutions Ltd

1

The most testing aspect of working with a world leader, I was discovering, is that their time is generally considered to be of more value than yours, which means that you are often left waiting upon their convenience. Appointments are abandoned at the last moment or are unexpectedly – and often quite aggressively – cut short by other people who believe their issues with the leader to be far more urgent than yours.

Obviously, I understood that the World Leader was going to have a great many things on his mind apart from his business with me, and so holding his attention for any prolonged period was always likely to be a challenge. What I was realising I had to learn if I wanted to work with such people – and despite all my qualms I was enjoying being granted a peek into this extraordinarily private and hidden world – was to always try to find ways to treat the inevitable down times philosophically and, whenever possible, to use them constructively. Imprisoned as I was within those palace walls, however, that was not easily achieved, which left me for hours with no distractions from the lead weight of misery that I was sentenced to carry around inside me. I craved constant distraction as desperately as any hopeless addict might crave the sweet oblivion of their drug of choice, and I knew that it would always be so, that there would never be any escape for me this side of the grave. I envied the World Leader his hectic level of constant activity, which I believed – perhaps presumptuously – left him no time to think, to reflect or to feel the agonies of regret that I was unable to escape from.

That was how I came to be strolling in that particular section of the palace gardens on that particular day, breathing in the sweet aroma of jasmine and enjoying the warmth of the sun. It was also how I had the time and the inclination to pause and speak to the sun-beaten old man in the wide-brimmed, white hat. Any conversation, however painful the language barrier might prove to be, was better than being left to the sadness of my own thoughts. He was pruning a small ornamental tree, squinting and humming as he worked, giving the job the same level of concentration as the Parisian hairdresser I had watched a few days earlier, working on the World Leader's hair. Good grooming, it seemed, was as important in a world leader's garden as it was in his personal appearance. The hairdresser, I noticed, had as much trouble keeping his client sitting still long enough for him to be able to do his work, as I was having. So many distractions, both human and over the telephone, so much jumping around, shouting and gesticulating. It was a wonder the World Leader didn't end up with his ear cut off. Maybe that was why they'd had to go all the way to Paris in order to find a man skilled enough to work safely with scissors under such challenging conditions. The gardener, I realised, was luckier than the hairdresser and me, being able to execute his craft in peace, away from the whirlwind that surrounded the man at the heart of the palace. He did not look like a man who feared being left alone with his thoughts.

So deeply immersed was he in his work that I was able to stand watching for several minutes before he looked up and saw me. The sharp snips of his small shears as they flashed across the leaves was the only sound to be heard above his quiet humming and the trickling of water as it moved through the various levels of the ponds, making the air feel a great deal cooler than it actually was. The thick, high, creeper-adorned walls rose around us, shutting out the chaos and danger that lay in the city streets beyond this private oasis and there seemed to be a lull in the explosions which had been going on all morning.

When he finally looked up and his eyes met mine they did not flinch away or show any of the self-consciousness or deference, or the hints of fear that I was coming to expect from a humble staff member in such a powerful man's house. He smiled with all the confidence of someone who takes for granted the fact that he is the equal of any man or woman.

"This is a beautiful garden," I said – an honest but unimaginative remark under the circumstances.

"Thank you," he replied and I immediately knew that language was not going to be a problem. "Would you like a guided tour?"

"I don't want to interrupt you."

"Not at all. I love showing people around. The admiration of others is one of the rewards for creating a garden."

He slotted his shears into a well-worn leather holster attached to his belt and gestured for me to join him on the other side of the ponds.

"Are you a gardener yourself?" he asked when I got to him.

"I have a garden," I said, feeling a stab of pain in my chest so fierce and sudden it took my breath away for a moment. "But I don't know if I would call myself a gardener exactly. Mostly I am just trying to keep it under control."

That wasn't entirely true, I had been obsessed with my garden, but I felt too intimidated by the scale of everything stretching out around me to even begin to explain my own philosophies on the subject. I wasn't even sure I still believed any of them any more anyway.

"That's pretty much all there is to it," he said. "Keeping things under control. Working with soil and plants. It's good for you."

"Good exercise you mean?"

"Good physical exercise, yes. But good mental exercise too. Good for the soul. A garden is a metaphor for life at almost every level. It is a close parallel to civilisation."

This was not the sort of conversation I had expected to find myself entering. I had expected to pass the time of day and maybe exchange a few pleasantries if we found we had a language in common. His English was fluent and quite heavily accented, but he did not sound like a local. He spoke like an educated man.

"Where are you from?" I asked, never able to stop myself from becoming the interrogator in any conversation, perhaps in the subconscious hope of diverting other people's attention before they had time to ask anything about me. I had always been my own least favourite subject and now there were so many areas of my life that I could not even start to talk about without risking the tears coming.

"Oh, so many places," he laughed, "but originally from Italy. That is where I created the garden which led to me being here. Mo saw my garden in Tuscany and fell in love with it. Everyone who sees it falls in love with it."

It took me a second to realise that when he said "Mo" he was referring to the World Leader. I was startled that a gardener should refer to his employer in such an informal manner, as if the two of them were old friends. I wondered if perhaps I had misunderstood and this man was a house guest like myself, a friend of the World Leader's family perhaps.

"Do you know Italy at all?" he asked.

"Yes," I pulled my thoughts back to the conversation. "I can imagine exactly the sort of garden you mean."

I knew enough to understand that the Italian garden has a long and noble history. Powerful people from emperors to popes have all contributed to the art form as patrons over the centuries. Now that I looked more closely at the landscape he was leading me through, I could see the Italian influence all around, in the use of water and symmetry and structure. But there were hints of other cultures too, whispers from the cool courtyards buried in North African cities and from monasteries perched on Far Eastern mountains. Round one corner a giant tranquil Buddha would sit inside a Chinese pavilion, overseeing a water garden, round another, Greek statues would frame a terrace or a gold-leafed swimming pool.

"We have imported architectural items from all over the world as well as plants and trees," he explained as we went from garden to garden. "All through history explorers have brought plants back home from foreign lands, but in the past they did not have the advantages of air travel. It was hard to keep plants alive on long, difficult sea voyages. So I think this must be the most globalised garden ever created."

"What do you mean exactly by gardens being a metaphor for civilisation?" I asked after a few quiet moments of staring around.

"Gardening separates us from the animals." He smiled and I waited for him to go on. I sensed that he had much more to say. It is my job, as well as my natural inclination, to listen while other people talk. Eventually he obliged. "We all start as simple

5

seeds. We are planted on Earth and we grow naturally, some of us thriving and some of us withering if left to the care of nature alone. Without gardeners the Earth would still be covered with beautiful places, places like forests and woodlands. We would still have mountain vistas, great lakes and jungles, but with judicious husbandry we have learned to control and improve and create things with the basic materials of nature – just as we have learned to modify and improve ourselves and our civilisations in every other way. Nature is beautiful but civilisation can improve upon that beauty."

"People have also created a great deal of destruction and ugliness," I said, unhappy to be reminded that some people's lives can wither even before they have had a chance to fully bloom.

"Not gardeners," he smiled. "Never gardeners. They might make mistakes, of course, but nature will mend them quickly, sometimes within a few months if there is some fertile soil and a temperate climate."

"Some things can never be mended," I said and instantly regretted it. He stopped walking and looked at me for a second before he spoke. I prayed he wouldn't ask me why I had said that.

"Everything is mended by the soil. You can have a battlefield covered in corpses and the next year you have a field of poppies. One day you have an African village piled high with the slaughtered bodies of the innocent and a few years later you have jungle once more."

He nodded down an avenue of carefully pleached trees, each one clipped into regimented uniformity, stretching maybe a hundred yards to a statue of the man whose garden we were standing in, like a guard of honour instructing us where to look, where to direct our obeisance.

"Just two simple lines," he said. "But no animal would ever create that."

A harassed looking figure bustled angrily out from behind the statue and started down the long path towards us. Infected by the old gardener's calmness I waited silently beside him as the figure drew closer and the crunching of the gravel grew more urgent beneath his highly polished shoes. I knew who it was and I raised my hand in a small display of greeting. He did not return the gesture, obviously wanting me to feel the full force of his annoyance. I guessed he had come to tell me that our master could spare me a few minutes of his time now, but that I must go with him immediately if I didn't want to miss the opportunity. There was always such an air of urgency around my employer and I felt strangely reluctant to leave the peace of the garden while at the same time welcoming the distracting, officious bustle of activity.

"You did not answer your phone," the man snapped when he reached us.

I pulled my phone out of my pocket to check. "Sorry," I said, "I forgot to turn it back on."

"Come quickly."

I followed obediently, aware that the old man was watching with amusement.

2

Despite the pace that the messenger set, by the time I reached the office someone else had already sneaked in to fill the few spare minutes of the leader's time that it had taken for me to get there from the garden. I hesitated in the doorway but he beckoned me in over the epaulet on his visitor's shoulder and gestured for me to sit in my usual chair. I fiddled with my recorder as I waited for him to dismiss the other man and sit down with me. I couldn't understand what they were talking about but their voices were raised in anger, maybe even tinged with a hint of barely suppressed fear, although such men would never admit to such an unmanly emotion.

"Sorry to have kept you waiting so long," he said as he finally perched on the edge of the sofa beside me, his dark, permanently narrowed eyes still on the screen of his mobile, manicured fingers flying across the keys. "My wife and daughters are shopping in Milan. They keep sending me pictures of dresses, asking me what I think," he gave a look of mock exasperation mixed, I suspected, with a tint of pride at the well documented beauty of his wife and girls. "What can you say about a dress?"

"That's okay," I said. "I've been enjoying your gardens. I was talking to one of your gardeners, a man with some interesting views."

He finally finished fiddling with the phone and looked at me as if taking in my words for the first time. "You were talking to a gardener?" he seemed to struggle with the concept for a moment and then a light appeared to go on. "Ah, you mean Lou?"

"He didn't tell me his name. An Italian gentleman."

He smiled for a second; flashing an unnaturally white and perfect set of teeth, as if I had brought to mind an amusing anecdote from his past. "You know, he comes from one of the oldest aristocratic families in Italy. We have known each other a long time." He paused for a second and I thought he was going to elaborate, but he pulled himself back to the business in hand and gestured that I should turn on my recorder.

"So," he snapped, "what else do you want to know?"

I tried to concentrate my attention on what he was saying, forcing my own thoughts to stay away and to keep him talking as coherently and honestly as possible. I didn't want to miss a single precious minute in case I wasn't given another chance. I wanted to hoover up as much information and as many quotes as possible, material that I could work on later in order to shape and build the book. He was able to keep interruptions away for nearly an hour, which was a record, before I was dismissed once more to the outer office and replaced by more grave-looking men in uniform. Once the door to the inner office was shut everyone bustled about their business and looked through me as if I didn't exist. Even though I had now been in the palace for nearly a fortnight I had no way of knowing if they had any idea why I was there, or indeed if they had any interest in finding out. Perhaps they had been told not to talk to me about my work, just as the lawyers had warned me not to talk to any of them, and so they could think of nothing else to say to me.

Knowing I wouldn't get any more time alone with him that day I went back to my bedroom for the few hours before dinner. I wanted to try again to get through to Caroline on Skype. Even though I knew how chilly her reaction to me would be, I longed to talk to her, to just see her familiar face, to reassure myself that she was still in my life. The palace people had ensured I had internet access and I could see that she was online, but when I pressed the dial button it just rang and rang. She was nearly always online, using the web to fill the dreadful, empty hours of her days. I could imagine her sitting at the other end, chewing her lip and staring at the screen and I hoped that if I kept ringing long enough she would become impatient and answer anyway, even though she had no wish to talk to me. At the same time part of me dreaded her picking up because I had no idea what we would talk about. It was bound to be a stilted and embarrassing conversation, but at least it would be contact of some sort. Eventually I had to accept that she was not going to pick up and I rang off with a mixture of relief and despair. I left my computer open on the bed beside me so that I could stare at the picture of her and Becky in the snow on my screensaver. Seeing them looking so happy as they laughed into the lens of my camera deepened my sadness, but I feared that if I snapped the computer shut on them I might sink so fast and deep into despair that my heart would actually break on the way down.

The silence was instant and oppressive as I lay there staring at their joyful faces. My chest was heavy with misery and I eventually forced myself to tear my eyes away for a few seconds and look around. If it hadn't been for the sick feeling that I now carried constantly in my stomach, the opulent luxury of the room would certainly have nauseated me. But it was beautiful too because of the way the late afternoon light hit the gold silk of the curtains and illuminated the gold leaf around the walls and the murals on the ceiling.

"My wife, Zana, designed the bedrooms," the leader had told me proudly at our first meeting after my arrival, when I was still searching for polite things to say and he had enquired if I was being made comfortable, like any good host. He became lost for a moment in his own memories. "Always when we were travelling together she would be examining the hotels where we stayed, the fabrics, the colours. Dubai, Bangkok, Paris, wherever we went she would always be researching, always taking pictures, always working. She has perfect taste."

Taste, of course is a personal thing, but what was unarguable was that the bed was so comfortable it made me feel guilty for even lying on it for a moment. I knew I didn't deserve such a pleasure, but it was still a pleasure none the less.

The urge to talk to Caroline, even if I didn't get a response, overcame me and I sat up to email her. It used to be so easy to write to her when we were apart, pages and pages of happy, love sick nonsense, but now there were so many subjects that I couldn't talk about, all of them the ones I longed to talk about more than anything. If I couldn't share my pain with her of all people, who could I share it with? I would have liked to describe every grotesque detail about being confined within the Court of Mo in the hope of making her laugh, or perhaps making her sigh with amazed disapproval, but I was aware the palace people might have some way of reading my emails, either by physically coming into the room when I was out or by intercepting them electronically in some way, so I had to stick to dry facts. I sent it all the same and felt slightly better.

That evening there was to be an official dinner in aid of a visiting dignitary, which I was aware was causing controversy in international diplomatic circles, although no one inside the palace wanted to admit it. As a result there were a number of places left vacant at the table at short notice and I had been informed that I would be expected to fill one of them. Since I had often ended up eating alone over the previous few days I welcomed the idea of a diversion. I'd had no appetite for months and it was easier to eat if there were other people around. I slept for a while before getting up to shower and dress.

When I went through to the banqueting hall from the crowded reception in the atrium, having swallowed two glasses of champagne from proffered silver trays, I didn't immediately recognise the elegant older gentleman that I had been seated next to. He seemed amused by my surprise when he greeted me like an old friend.

"I asked to be seated with you," he grinned, "I hope you don't mind. I thought you seemed like someone who needed to talk a little more. My name is Lou." He held out his hand and I laughed to cover my embarrassment at failing to recognise him in his evening finery.

As we sat down I noticed him wink at someone across the table. I followed his gaze to a beautiful young woman who appeared to be smiling back with genuine warmth and I felt envious of both of them for having such a connection. It reminded me how lonely I felt.

"That is Claudia," he explained when he saw me looking, "my wife. Isn't she lovely?"

"Indeed," I felt slightly embarrassed to have been caught admiring someone so obviously attractive.

"I owe her everything. She has opened my eyes to so much in life that is worthwhile. I could not believe it when she first showed an interest in me. I met her in this very house. Do you know what she did?"

"No," I couldn't imagine what might be coming next.

"She took my hand in hers – such a light, delicate touch – and led me through the garden to stand in front of one of the oldest trees here, an olive tree with a trunk that has been gnarled and twisted by at least a century of growth and worn by the adversity of the weather patterns, the burning of the winds and the sun and the biting cold of the winter nights. Its short branches had been so carefully and lovingly pruned by the gardeners that it had a lush covering of silver leaves. 'I think there is much more beauty to admire there than in any young sapling', was all she said."

I guessed from the flowery way he told the story that he had told it many times before, elaborating and polishing it until it had become a perfect little fable to justify his marriage to a beautiful woman half his age.

"It seems saplings can show wisdom too," I said and was rewarded with a bellow of genuine laughter that cut through the tense quietness that seemed to have surrounded most of the table and made a number of smart heads turn towards us in alarmed surprise. I noticed that most of the men were wearing dress uniforms adorned with medals and gold braid which made them look like players from a military musical, something by Gilbert and Sullivan perhaps. There were so many more questions that I wanted to ask my new friend, but as our first course was served my attention was taken by an over-dressed and over-jewelled woman sitting on my other side who wanted to talk about the food and seemed to have imbibed even more champagne than I had. I was forced to be patient until it was polite to turn back to Lou. Glancing at the end of the table as I listened to her I could see that Mo was distracted by his own thoughts, neither eating the food in front of him nor listening to the elderly woman who was talking to him. His eyes were flickering around the table as if he hoped to listen in on every conversation, as if he was anxious that others might be whispering about him, that they might be plotting behind his back. Aides would slide up behind him every so often and murmur things into his ear that would make him drum his fingers on the table with poorly disguised exasperation. He looked as if he was using every ounce of self control he possessed to hold himself back from exploding.

"So," I said once I had Lou's attention again, "do you work all the time in the gardens here?"

"I am tending the gardens all the time but I have to say it never feels like work. What I used to do felt like work."

"What did you used to do?"

"I was in business, you know how it is. That is how I came to be here. Mo and I were doing business together a lot for many years, even before he became so eminent. We got on so well that when his time came to lead the country he asked if I would be his assistant. I have to tell you, that was hard work. Mo works like a damned fool, but perhaps it makes him happier than not working would. Some people do not like to be left alone with their thoughts."

He took a mouthful of food and looked at me as if hoping I would take the bait and say something. I didn't, even though he had hit the target dead centre, and after a moment he finished his mouthful and continued.

"It was Claudia who persuaded me that there were better things to do than worry about profits and protocol all day long. She discovered my 'inner gardener'!" Another bellow of merriment. "And between us we talked Mo into letting me change jobs. He still grumbles about it, still tries to make me come back inside the palace. I made him a great deal of money over the years."

"Do you not miss the excitement?"

"It no longer interests me. I would rather spend my remaining days with Claudia and the children. And with the plants of course."

I could understand that. "How did you persuade him then?"

"He had visited my garden in Italy many times, as my guest. My mother lived with me then and she treated him like a second son. He was not used to so much love coming from the background that he did. I could see that he was at peace whenever he was walking or sitting in the gardens. I promised him I could give him the same peace of mind outside his own back door. Of course he says he hardly ever has time to come outside, but I tell him that is his own fault! The garden is always there, it is him who is missing."

"So, did you know his father?" I asked.

"Oh yes, as much as you can ever know a man like that. I knew the whole family because Mo would treat me like a brother whenever I was staying with him."

"And you think he did not receive love?"

He smiled, as if to let me know that he understood that I was using him for research. "I am sure he and his father loved and respected one another in the end, but I don't remember ever hearing either of them say a kind word to the other. I never saw them embrace beyond perhaps a handshake for the cameras. Being Italian that seemed strange to me at first, but over the years I have met other families like Mo's and I don't think the relationship was unusual. He was sent abroad to school when he was still very young. Such things have an effect, don't you think?"

At the end of dinner there were some formal and slightly embarrassed speeches from people who obviously wanted to remain on good terms with Mo but didn't want to say anything that might later be used to prove they had praised him too much.

"Diplomats and politicians," Lou muttered in my ear during one particularly non-committal speech, "blowing with the wind. No substance, no beliefs, no real friendships."

Mo obviously didn't believe a word any of them were saying, never looking as if he was listening to any of the speakers, always tapping his fingers or whispering to the lackeys who bent down to gain his ear. Eventually the speakers had all run dry and they turned to their host to respond. It seemed for a moment as if he hadn't realised that the whole table was looking at him expectantly, but eventually he spoke with a deep, throaty rumble which suggested relief at the ordeal of the meal being over.

"Okay," he said. "Now we go for some entertainment."

With no further ceremony he stood and marched out through the double doors which were swept open for him. Outside there was another gaggle of uniformed men waiting to talk to him. By the time I and Lou were walking out Mo seemed to have finished listening to them and joined us. To my surprise he put his arm round my shoulder and laughed loudly.

"So, my writer friend, are you looking forward to the concert? They are my wife's favourite. She is very sad that she is not here to see them. When they were booked things were going to be different."

I had heard that a boyband who had emerged from a reality talent contest had been flown over to give a concert and I had caught sight of some rather nervous looking teenage boys being escorted about the palace on my way down to the dinner. Gold chairs had been laid out for us to sit on but Mo stayed standing at the back so that his aides could continue whispering in his ear and he seemed to expect me to stand with him. Lou sat with Claudia who looked entirely serene and unconnected from the nervous atmosphere that surrounded us. The poor boys did their best to whip the audience up into the sort of hysterical state they had obviously grown used to experiencing since being catapulted to television fame, but most of the audience seemed more interested in talking to one another or craning their necks to see what Mo was doing at the back of the room. The noise of the music and the frenetic lighting show made it impossible for anyone to hear anything properly, adding to their apparent paranoia. Mo left the show before it finished and didn't reappear. Waiters arrived to hand round more drinks as the unhappy looking boyband was replaced by more traditional local musicians and the obviously relieved crowd were able to talk more easily amongst themselves once more. I noticed that Lou and Claudia had also disappeared.

I tried to ensure that I drank enough to make the thought of returning to my room alone at the end of the evening bearable, but not so much that I ran the risk of making a fool of myself while still in company. I had noticed that many of the guests had drunk virtually nothing and assumed that many of the ones in uniform were still on duty. By the time I was finally back on my giant, cushion-strewn bed it was late, but the alcohol had loosened my inhibitions and I decided to try to Skype Caroline again. It was probably just as well that she didn't answer because I would undoubtedly have burst into tears at the sight of her and there would have been nothing in the world she could have said that would have made me feel any better. The drink made it possible for me to fall asleep mercifully quickly.

3

It was not unusual to wake up and see smoke rising from somewhere outside the palace walls, often preceded by an explosion, but it was surprising to see it billowing up only a hundred yards away from my window as I pulled back my bedroom curtains the following morning. More surprising still was the apparent lack of concern anyone was showing. Normally when anything unexpected happened anywhere close to the palace there would be men in dark suits running around talking into phones or walkie-talkies. Sometimes there would even be groups of armed soldiers with heavy boots and faces obscured by helmets and darkened visors, but everything in the garden below seemed tranquil and there was no sign of people anywhere as the smoke drifted up into the cloudless blue sky.

An hour or so later, having been served a lavish breakfast in an eerily quiet dining room, I was informed that Mo, (how quickly I had started to imitate my new friend from the garden, inside my head at least), would not be free to talk to me until after lunch because he had somewhere else to go which was important enough to require him being lifted from the palace roof in a helicopter. I went out into the garden with the remains of my coffee and saw that there was still smoke coming from behind some high hedges. I made my way towards where I thought the source would be and found Lou leaning on the handle of his fork, watching the bonfire burn out.

"Good morning," he said when he saw me. "Has Mo stood you up again?"

"I'm used to it. You have a good fire going there. I thought we had been bombed in the night when I saw the smoke."

"There's something very satisfying about building a successful fire," he said, pushing a few stray branches into the flames with his fork. "I think I get almost as much satisfaction from it as I used to get from putting together successful deals, or successfully launching projects. It's the same principles really."

I laughed and he looked up from his labours with one eyebrow raised. "I'm sorry," I said, "is this another of your gardening metaphors?"

He thought for a moment. "Yes," he said eventually. "I guess it is. To create a successful fire you need to lay the foundations carefully, with all the lightest and most combustible materials at the bottom. What is that phrase, something about a line of ducks?"

"Having all your ducks in a row?" I suggested.

"Exactly so. If everything is well planned and well prepared, the timing is right and all your ducks are, indeed, 'in a row', then the flames will take hold very quickly. If the material is a little too green and unready, or if you build it carelessly and too quickly, it won't work. That doesn't mean you shouldn't keep trying to get it going, but it will probably just flare up and then die away, or it will smoulder on for days without really getting going. I think it is the same with business deals and projects, don't you? Most people don't lay the foundations correctly because they are too impatient or too greedy or too stupid – or perhaps they simply can't afford to take the time and so they just have to do the best they can with limited resources. With experience you learn how to prepare the fire correctly to get the best result."

In the past I would not have been particularly interested in talk about business deals or making money. It had never been a subject that had bothered me or Caroline and we had actively disapproved of anyone who seemed to put too much emphasis on such things. In the years we had lived together in London we had become increasingly bored with the endless talk about rising house prices, obscene salaries and deals that seemed to excite everyone else around us at the dinner parties we were invited to. It sometimes felt that we were the only people in the world who didn't care about "climbing the ladder" and getting rich. Now that had all changed and I was more desperate than anyone for any tips on how to make substantial sums of money. Being the provider of a large amount of financial support was the only possible way that I could justify my continued existence on the planet. It was the reason I had agreed to travel all this way and be incarcerated within the palace walls at Mo's beck and call when every part of me yearned to be somewhere else. Contrary to all my previous beliefs, becoming rich had now become my main purpose in life. It was as if I was travelling in exactly the opposite direction to Lou and I was anxious to milk him of all his accrued wisdom as quickly as I could before he passed on by.

"So, most of us just go through life in a state of slow smoulder then?" I said. "With the occasional flare-ups if we're lucky?"

He stared at me thoughtfully. "I think you might be

mocking me," he said after a few moments. "But yes, I think that works as a metaphor, don't you?"

I sipped my coffee and stood beside him for a while, both of us hypnotised by the last of the flames. Eventually he spoke again.

"And if you want to build a business that is going to continue, you need to ensure you have plenty more fuel waiting to go on the fire. If your supplies dwindle then the fire will die away. That is what happens with so many deals and why leaders like Mo have to rush around the whole time trying to keep the fires stoked when they should in fact walk away and start again with a new plan, make fresh preparations and lay proper foundations. If you try to keep a fire going for its own sake, just like keeping a business going because you can't bear to see it end, sooner or later it is going to become a waste of your time and energies."

"Is that what Mo is having to do then? Just fire fighting?"

"All leaders have to do it, because their people expect it of them and because when they take power they inevitably inherit many existing and poorly planned fires. Some of these fires may be dearly loved by people who matter and any leader who allows them to go out on their watch is going to be blamed by the people who trusted them with the job. That is why they eventually have to start telling lies, because it is an impossible task, but they can never admit that. No fire can be kept going forever, they all dwindle and die eventually, like businesses, like empires, like political regimes."

"Like lives," I said. He looked at me as if expecting me to explain what I meant, so I changed the subject quickly. "Do you think Mo's regime is dwindling?"

"Do you not read the international media?"

"Do you tell him these things?"

"I used to try, but he didn't want to hear because he knows its true and he believes there is nothing he can do to change the way things are. He used to have to listen to me because I was with him nearly all the time. Now he avoids me if he thinks I am going to start lecturing him."

"All world leaders should probably listen more to what they are being told by disinterested parties, shouldn't they?"

"But interested parties tend to shout the loudest, I'm afraid," he said, "drowning the rest of us out."

He scraped the last of the branches onto the fire and then put down his fork. "Come, let's find somewhere cooler to sit."

Although I wasn't sure whether it would be wise to admit it, I had been watching some of the events going on outside the palace walls on television during the long hours when I had nothing to do other than go back to my room and wait for Mo to have some more time for me. I had felt a little like a naughty schoolboy accessing adult channels in his bedroom, my finger poised above the off button, ready to press if anyone knocked on the door. I was aware that it was possible the room was bugged, so I kept the volume low, following in subtitles wherever possible.

The incident which had set the fuse burning had happened the day after I arrived at the palace. It had not been in the city, but several hundred miles away in a sand-blown village which didn't look like it had yet been touched by modern conveniences like electricity or running water. It seemed to start with a disagreement between local sheep herders and officials of the government's oil exploration company. The oil men had the backing of some soldiers who appeared to panic in the face of a small angry mob waving sticks and throwing stones in order to drive the oil men off a disputed piece of barren land. Presumably the soldiers were used to operating in such areas with impunity, confident that they were out of sight of anyone who would report back on their activities to the media. They had opened fire with a shocking casualness, some of them even laughing like they were competing to shoot rabbits, unaware that someone in the village had a mobile phone and knew how to use it. The resulting footage of the carnage amongst the dust clouds quickly made its way from YouTube onto CNN and from there onto virtually every news channel in the world.

It was the sort of clip that no editor could resist, depicting a scene that seared itself onto the memory; simple, unarmed village people being gunned down by highly professional looking soldiers who were behaving like a hunting party, and who then proceeded to beat the fallen boys and men with the butts of the guns that had brought them down. The screamed abuse and babbled prayers of the village women added a heart breaking backing track to the shocking pictures.

There had been many smooth diplomats rolled out into studios around the world to express their horror at the scenes and to assure the world that investigations would be made into how such a thing could have happened and to ensure that it never happened again. But the damage was done. The world's media spotlight was now shining onto Mo's regime and its past record and people all over the country were watching the clips and realising they were not alone in their dissatisfaction with the way they were being treated. Experts in the history of the area and its politics agreed that when he first came to power Mo had been a liberal and liberating force after the many dark decades of his father's reign. For many years he was able to trade on that initial wave of international goodwill. He was widely liked by other world leaders who had come and gone during his time in power, and the media's attention had been distracted by other less attractive and more openly aggressive world leaders. Suddenly the media was suggesting that it was time to take another look at what had been going on while they were looking the other way, and a spiral of negative publicity had started to spin downwards, totally out of control. All this I was aware of, but I had not thought it wise to speak out loud about it within the confines of the palace. It was like I was constantly holding my breath until the next instalment of my agreed fee made its way safely into my bank account.

4

Lou and I sat quietly for a while under the shade of a vine, watching one of the other gardeners methodically brushing the already pristine paths around the fish ponds.

"When I started working here they used to use all sorts of mechanical devices," he said, "but I made them give them away. Wherever you went in the garden you would hear electric cutters or strimmers and God alone knows what else. There was never any peace or tranquillity."

"Didn't the gardeners mind losing their labour saving devices?"

"One of two of them were furious. In fact they petitioned all the way up to Mo himself."

"What did he say?"

"Mainly he wanted to know how I had managed to cause so much trouble for him so quickly when he thought he had put me out to grass. I reminded him that half the country was out of work and that in one fell swoop I had created a need for at least a dozen more workers to do things by hand in the traditional ways. He ranted on for a bit about me being anti-progress and trying to take his people back to the Dark Ages, but he could see I wasn't listening and eventually he ran out of steam."

"And did the workforce come round to the idea?"

"Many of them had sons or nephews or grandfathers who needed extra employment. It wasn't hard to sell them the idea of hiring them, with the result that a pleasant family atmosphere grew up quite quickly, a feeling of continuity which the previous few years had done great damage to. Progress is good in many, many ways, but sometimes it is better to do things slowly and quietly. People need something to do with their days."

I was just savouring the tranquillity that he was talking about when it was interrupted by the swelling throb of several helicopters approaching and landing back on the roof of the palace, the wind from their blades bending the trees and making the surfaces of the ponds shimmy at our feet. Once their engines had been killed the silence was palpable.

"I guess that means he's back," I said, pulling out my phone to ensure I had remembered to switch it on should they want to summon me into his presence.

"Let's go and find Claudia," Lou said, ignoring my comment and standing up. "She wants to meet you."

I was pretty confident that I wouldn't be needed inside the palace for a while yet since everyone seemed to have far more pressing matters on hand than the leader's autobiography, and I liked the idea of seeing where Lou and Claudia lived. I followed him down a long avenue of towering palm trees and through a low, studded gate in a high wall, which looked as if it might have been there at least a thousand years. Inside was a replica of an English Georgian stable block, which appeared to have been converted into houses for palace workers. The door to one of the houses stood open and as we approached I could hear the sounds of women's laughter and foreign tongues coming from inside. The noise didn't stop as we walked into the kitchen. Claudia was standing at the table, preparing food with an older woman as two small girls ran around their legs. She was just as striking without her evening finery, her brow glistening with sweat and her eyes sparkling from the laughter she and the other woman were sharing. She proffered her cheek for Lou to peck as he walked past her and sank into a chair which stood by another door open to a courtyard beyond, indicating a chair for me.

"Hello," Claudia said to me with a welcoming smile. "Nice to see you again. Lou tells me you are writing a book for Mo."

"I'm supposed to be," I said. I assumed that since I hadn't mentioned it to anyone, Mo must have told Lou, which made it okay to admit it. "But he seems to have a lot on his plate."

"This is Sanka," Lou gestured to the other woman, who nodded but did not attempt to communicate. I suspected we did not have a common language. "She is Claudia's mother, and a great woman."

Claudia seemed to be translating this comment for her mother, who merely shrugged, neither agreeing nor disagreeing with the description.

"And these are the two most wicked girls in the world," he went on as the excited children leapt onto his lap the moment he was settled. I turned away for a moment to compose myself and when I turned back I saw that Lou had noticed my reaction. He looked puzzled but obviously knew better than to ask if I was all right.

Claudia interrupted whatever she was doing in order to pour us coffee and then she and her mother followed the children out into the courtyard to sit in the sun.

"You have a lovely family," I said as we watched them play through the open door and once I felt I could trust my voice not to crack.

"I am blessed. Claudia and Sanka suffered a great deal in their homeland and I have been able to bring them at least a few years of safety and contentment. You cannot hope to do more than that for people who have the misfortune to be born in troubled times and troubled places. The village that they came from was destroyed by soldiers. Sanka's mother was one of the villagers killed for refusing to leave her home, and that was just weeks after her husband and father were killed simply for being men."

I realised that my hand had involuntarily come up to cover my mouth at the picture he was painting with his matter–of–fact description of the horror. He was watching me closely again as he continued to talk and I tried to compose myself better.

"Stability and security," he shrugged, "they are just illusions. But they are necessary illusions because without them there would be no way of going on. Without them we would be returned to the state of being nervous wild animals, always alert for the scent and sound of predators. That would be no way to live. That would not be civilisation. To have civilisation you have to feel secure to move forward, to think and to dream. We must all cling to our delusions."

We fell back into silence for a few moments, both lost in our own thoughts.

"That was how Claudia came to be here," he resumed after a while. "Floating like pollen in search of more fertile soil. Someone had to make money in order for her mother and other surviving family members to survive. She was lucky to be blessed with great beauty and she was invited to meet Mo. Mo likes to have beautiful people around him. It is his weakness, I suppose you could say."

So, Claudia and I had both ended up here for much the same

reasons. I couldn't help but admire the way she had built a new life from her tragedy, and to envy her seeming contentment. I knew I would never be able to do that.

"I have heard people say that about him," I replied non-committally. "So she came here of her own free will?"

"Mo may have some faults," he laughed, "but he is not a slave trader. Yes, she came of her own accord. It was a 'business decision' you might say. Believe me, when you have seen your home burned to the ground and your family killed, you know that there are worse fates than living in a beautiful palace like this, with guards on the gates and food in the kitchens. Mo is a little like a gardener of people. Someone else might find a beautiful plant in another country and have it sent over to plant in their own garden. I have certainly done that many times in the past. Mo likes to do the same with people. He nurtures them well and they flourish as a result. Claudia met me and once I got to know her story I suggested that Sanka should come over here to live with us as well."

"Why did the soldiers destroy the village?"

He didn't answer immediately but I didn't interrupt the silence, quite happy to wait for an answer. I was only half listening to his voice anyway, my head spinning with my own thoughts. For the first time he seemed reluctant to answer one of my questions spontaneously and directly. It seemed I had reached the outer edges of his candour.

"There were business interests involved," he said eventually. "The villagers had the misfortune to live in the path of a potentially profitable pipeline. I think that it should have been feasible to build them a better village a little way away, but other people decided that it would be quicker to simply force them out with virtually no compensation. There are many unkind people in the world."

He fell silent again, staring into his coffee cup as if it provided a window into the past.

"Is that part of what decided you to become a gardener?" I asked, wanting to restart him talking. The girls were running round and round the courtyard outside, shouting with the joy of being alive and I was feeling fearful that one of them would trip and I would have to witness her pain as she hit the hard cobblestones. I wanted to shout at them to slow down but I knew that would be inappropriate. I knew that the agitation which I could feel rising inside me was ridiculous, but I wasn't confident I could control it.

"I have never met a cruel plant, if that is what you mean," he smiled. "So I suppose in a way the answer is yes. It was like many things coming together at once. I could see what was happening to other people around Mo, and I didn't want that to happen to me. Then there was Claudia's influence, and seeing what had happened to her family and their village."

"Had you been married before?"

"No," he said. "I was always too busy, always travelling, always working. It wouldn't have been fair on any woman. It wouldn't have been fair on any children I might have had. As it is I can give the girls as much of my day as they might want. It was worth waiting for. I spent a lot of time getting the soil right before I actually planted my seeds."

He laughed, delighted by his own joke, as if he had only just thought of it, but I suspected it was one he had used many times before.

5

"How did you first meet Mo?" I asked after we had been sitting peacefully for a while.

"Always working, aren't you?" he chuckled. "Always thinking."

"It's a curse," I replied, "Always being curious."

"You don't mean that. You mean it is a blessing and you are right. If you don't ask questions you cannot move forward, you cannot learn."

"So, how did you first meet?"

"You don't like talking about yourself, Mr Ghostwriter, do you?"

"I'd rather learn something new." I was annoyed to feel myself blushing and my throat closing up as if wanting to stop me from saying any more. I was sure he was beginning to see inside my head, able to somehow uncover things that I was trying hard to hide from myself as well as the rest of the world. He was teasing me and I didn't like it. "Something I don't already know."

"Well, you're right. It is interesting how we first met, and not what you would expect, I'm sure. I will show you something."

He got up and delved into the pocket of a coat hanging on a nearby hook, pulling out an early model iPod and untangling the white wires of the headphones as he sat back down, squinting at the tiny screen as he worked it clumsily with thumbs hardened by soil and hand tools.

"Claudia gave me this," he said. "She thought that I could use it when I garden."

"Do you?"

"Not if it is quiet. I prefer the silence. But if there is a lot of noise going on beyond the walls, shooting and explosions, then it provides an escape route back to serenity, back to my own thoughts. I have heard enough shooting in my life."

He put one of the earphones into his ear as he fiddled with the controls, frowning with the concentration of a man not practised in the digital arts.

"Okay," he said eventually, passing the earphones across to me. "Listen to that."

My head was filled with the plaintive tones of Scott McKenzie, urging those heading for San Francisco to wear flowers in their hair.

"So what year do you think that would have been, then?" he asked when the song finished and I passed the earphones back. "1967, maybe? The same sort of time as The Beatles released Sgt Pepper's Lonely Heart Club Band?"

"I would guess around there," I said, startled by this unexpected change of subject. They were not images I expected him to hold in his head. "We could easily find out."

"It doesn't matter exactly. But that song was everywhere, all over the world, and that was where I first met Mo."

"In San Francisco?"

"Yes, and that song was actually playing at the time. We were both following the hippie trail, searching for something, both disappointed by the other people we were meeting there but excited at starting out on adult life at the same time, excited by the idea of free love and music."

I tried to imagine the two old men that I was meeting as young hippies. This was not a part of Mo's life that anyone else had mentioned to me so far, not part of the official biographical details that the palace public relations people handed out. The Minister had certainly not given me any sign that he knew about Mo before he was President. I was pretty sure if I wrote about it they would censor it out of the eventual manuscript, but it was still interesting, giving another dimension to the grim faced world leader whose haggard features were gracing the covers of so many magazines and leading so many television news bulletins around the world. It was hard to imagine that he had once been young and free of care. I couldn't even imagine him in a place like San Francisco, mixing with ordinary people.

"Are there any photographs of you from that period?"

"Of me, or of Mo?"

"Either."

"I will look and see what I can find."

"Did you have any idea who he was when you met? Did you know who his family were?"

"No, we didn't talk about such things. His family were angry with him for being a rebel. He had run away from home and they were looking for him, so he couldn't trust anyone. Has he not told you any of this?"

"No, nothing."

"Mo is exceptionally good at keeping secrets."

I was aware of that. The world's media speculated a great deal about secret torture chambers beneath the palace, into which political enemies would disappear forever, but Mo never gave a flicker of an indication as to whether he knew anything about such things. When I had asked him about the rumours he brushed them aside as if they were too ridiculous to even contemplate, as if they were just media fantasies dreamed up by his enemies in order to discredit him in the eyes of the world. All my experience of working with the victims of torture and oppressive regimes told me that whether he personally knew about it or not, most of the rumours were likely to be true, but I couldn't let myself think about it. I had agreed to look at things from his side, not the side that I would normally have been looking from. I was writing his story, not the stories of whatever poor wretches there might be locked away underground. At moments when I came close to thinking about such things, it felt like my head was going to split open.

"I just knew that he was fun to be with," Lou continued, "and much more intelligent than most of the people hanging out on the free love scene. I was a student exploring the world a little, I was not a dedicated hippy, and I could tell he was the same. I knew nothing about world politics at that time. I don't think I even knew what country he came from. We spent a summer together, just experimenting with life."

"And you stayed friends from then on?"

"No, we both went back to our normal lives and it was about ten years before our paths crossed again. He was doing deals by then on behalf of his country and his father, beginning to make a mark for himself, back in the family and being groomed for leadership. I was also establishing myself in business, trying to make some money. I went for an appointment with someone who I was told was important to a deal I wanted to set up and I found my old friend waiting for me. We had both changed a great deal by then; no long hair, sharp suits. He was as surprised as I was when I walked into his office and from then on we did everything together. It has been like a sort of love affair I suppose."

Claudia came back in to offer us food and smiled when she saw he was holding the iPod. "You like the same music as Lou?" she asked me.

"He's much younger than me," Lou answered on my behalf.

"It has been so interesting for me to find all the music from his youth," she went on, ignoring his interruption. "Most of it I had never heard in my country and so I felt like I was discovering it in the same way that he had done when he was young. Those songs, like Bridge over Troubled Water?" She glanced at Lou who nodded. "They are important parts of his culture. Important songs, no?"

I was still trying to imagine Mo, in beard, beads and caftan maybe, listening to the sort of songs that stirred a whole generation, just like any other young man rebelling against a strict and controlled background, dreaming dreams, hoping to find a better way to live.

"All you need is love," Lou said with one of his characteristic bellows of laughter. "It took me more than thirty years to fully appreciate the truth of those words."

Claudia ruffled his thick white hair affectionately and set about making us food.

6

The next morning Mo beckoned me in impatiently when he saw me loitering in the outer office to his sanctum.

"We need this book to happen fast," he said. "You must have enough material now to write. You need to tell the world the truth about what is happening here, to end all these rumours, all this propaganda. Can you write it now?"

"No, not yet," I said, horrified that he imagined I could spin an entire book out of the few pat biographical details he had shared with me so far.

"So, what else do you need to know?"

"Well, I need to know about your past. For instance, Lou was telling me about your time together in San Francisco. I knew nothing about that."

"San Francisco?" He looked puzzled, as if struggling to be able to remember that far back, to a time when he must have been a very different person. "Lou has told you about San Francisco?"

"A little, but I would like to hear your version of those times."

"Lou talks a lot of crap," he snapped. "He can afford to. He doesn't have my responsibilities."

"What made you want to go out there?" I persisted despite being troubled that I might have been indiscreet and that Lou would now be in trouble.

"To San Francisco?" He was obviously having difficulty imagining why I would be interested in something which was so far from the reality of his present situation. His life before coming to power held no interest for him and so he couldn't imagine why it would interest me or anyone else. His eyes flickered up towards a group of uniformed men who were hovering with barely disguised agitation in the open doorway. "We will have to do this later."

"I'm available if you have the time," I said as I was hurried out by the men coming in.

"I will make the time," he assured me, "This is important, we need to explain things to people. Keep your phone switched on, so you can be found quickly."

I did as he said and walked out into the garden in the hope of bumping into Lou and in need of clear, fresh air. The level of noise outside the walls had risen and there were more soldiers than usual at the gates, all of them showing the same sense of agitation I had seen in the military leaders inside. I had seen a news bulletin on the television in my room while I was dressing, with a film of the streets the previous night, lit by burning cars and by people setting light to posters of Mo's face. There had been crowds of young people running, leaving fallen bodies in their wake as they tried to avoid the pursuing police bullets, batons and smoke bombs. Most of them had been men with their faces half covered in scarves, but there had been some courageous-looking women amongst them too. There had been some old footage shown of Mo smiling and making speeches, but nothing new, no coherent, reassuring message from a leader still in control. It was no wonder he wanted to do something about his image in the eyes of the world, but a book was probably going to take too long, particularly since he had so little time to even talk to me. I had a horrible feeling that I would inevitably fail him, but if I could just get one more of the fat, unreal payments safely into my bank account before that happened.

Lou was listening to his iPod in order to cut out the gunfire and explosions as he pruned and didn't hear me until I put a hand on his shoulder. He pulled the earphones out and straightened up. We both stood listening to the noises for a few moments.

"Are things a bit jumpy in there?" he asked, gesturing towards the palace.

"More than a bit. I thought it would be more peaceful out here."

"It may be getting close to the time when Mo should think about going." He seemed to be talking more to himself than to me.

"Where would he go?"

"I don't know. We haven't had that conversation. There are a lot of countries that would still accept him if he stepped aside now. If the troops and the police kill too many more people it will become harder for anyone to be seen as his friend and protector. It's not in his nature though, to run away. He sees himself as the centre of the family, the 'fortune generator' you might say. He wouldn't like the idea of ever retiring to the sidelines."

"The family must have enough money to support themselves in exile, surely."

"Undoubtedly. That is a conversation I have had with him many times over the years, particularly when he was trying to dissuade me from giving up work and coming out here to prune the roses. He couldn't understand how anyone could decide they had enough money and would give up pursuing it. He just couldn't grasp it. To him it would be like giving up on life. It isn't easy changing your mindset after being set on one path for so long."

"So how does anyone decide they have enough?" I asked, wanting to ask him more specifically about himself but not quite having the nerve without the licence of being his ghostwriter.

"You mean how did I decide I had enough?"

"Yes," I grinned sheepishly. "Would you have called yourself a 'fortune generator'?"

"Most certainly. It was necessary that I become one. There hadn't been one in my family for several generations. My father and grandfather never needed to make money, they could just be caretakers of the family homes and lands that my great grandfather had built up. He was our last fortune generator and the resources he created had ebbed away with time – and careless handling. My father enjoyed gardening just like me, but he didn't take the precaution of building capital first. He didn't know how to, most people don't. Most people who belong to rich families earn very little themselves, but if there is a fortune generator at the centre they can keep the machine turning over so that everyone has enough of what they need. Everyone around them then finds another role, as a carer of children, a decorator or a maintainer of homes and any small income that they make they can keep for themselves because all the big expenses, like the houses and family travel or education expenses have already been taken care of. Others can earn small livings from providing services to these families. Some of them may even think they are earning a lot for what they do. They may be perfectly satisfied with the situation. It has always been so. If everyone in a family has to work for a wage – or even half of them – then the family is never really going to live well. Most people feel quite well disposed towards fortune generators, even left wing people. They may have different ideas on how we should spend our money but they don't begrudge us the fruits of our labours if they can see we support and nourish an extended network – as long as they feel we have laboured productively in the first place."

Without even asking he was already leading me back towards his house for coffee. It was as if he had read my mind again and knew that I wanted another dose of the warm family atmosphere that filled his kitchen, even if it did make me want to weep when I actually thought about it. He probably assumed that the noise and agitation all around the palace compound was rubbing off on me, making me nervous and uncertain what I was doing there, and perhaps it was. I was unsure whether I was being reckless to stay there – or was I being brave, doing the job I had been hired for regardless of the danger? Was I just being avaricious for the money? Did I have any of my old social conscience left? I no longer felt able to judge such things having been proved so tragically inept at making good judgements in the past.

"So what marks some people out as fortune generators then?" I asked, hoping that he would describe some characteristic that I would be able to spot in myself.

"There has to be a need. I could see that my family were about to lose everything if I didn't generate a large amount of capital. My parents would have had to leave the house they had lived in all their lives, or at least my father had and my mother had been there since she was sixteen. So, I had an urgent need. There must be a sense of urgency before anything can ever happen."

I nodded to show my understanding of what he was saying because I definitely had an urgent need.

"I also needed to prove something to my father. I think perhaps everyone who achieves anything needs to prove something to someone."

I nodded again, but as I thought of Caroline I felt another of the stabs of pain which punctuated all my waking hours, remembering the looks of contempt that had replaced the love I had once believed I could see shining out of her eyes whenever she looked at me. I definitely wanted to prove to her that I could still achieve something good, that I could at least go a little way towards repairing the terrible damage I had done to all our lives.

"They need to be able to take risks, perhaps even to relish them. They have to be prepared to lose everything."

I had always taken risks, but never in pursuit of wealth, more out of idleness and carelessness. I wasn't stupid but I did stupid things which I could often see with hindsight had been risky. Was that the same thing? I hadn't been even remotely prepared to lose everything in the way I had.

"If you make a fortune you can achieve a sort of immortality, at least for a little longer than the usual span of a life. My great grandfather extended his mortality a couple of hundred years or so because of his achievements. He is still talked about now in some circles, but few people talk of my father or grandfather. Most fortune generators are striving to achieve something like that."

That certainly didn't apply to me. I wanted nothing more than to slide quietly out of the world and to be forgotten would have felt like a mercy. I would even have facilitated my own exit if I hadn't known that I had to at least try to make things better and easier for Becky and Caroline and the rest of our family before I went.

"What sort of business deals did you and Mo do before he took over running the country?" I asked once we were sitting in the kitchen. I saw Lou exchange a look with Claudia which suggested that he might again be about to give a less than open answer.

"A man who is going to run a country needs many things in order to hold onto power. We worked out what those things were and made them happen."

"A man needs a fortune to hold onto power?"

"That is the first thing he needs. He needs other things too, like authority and the ability to enforce his will. Many of these things can be bought with a fortune, some of them can't."

7

When I was told I had the job of writing Mo's autobiography it felt for a moment as if it was meant to be, like some sort of destiny. Just at a moment when I needed money more desperately than I had ever needed it before I was being offered the highest paying job I had ever had. It was an absurd amount of money for the time I would actually be investing in the project. Money had never been any sort of driving force for me in the past, beyond the obvious need to be able to eat and keep a roof over my head. Whenever one of my books had become a bestseller and I had shared in the rewards it had always been a wonderful bonus, but never something to be relied upon or planned for. What I always looked for, what excited me, were stories that interested me. I loved to listen to people who knew something I didn't and who I felt deserved to be given voices in the wider world. When I was successful in giving them those voices, the satisfaction was complete. While Mo was undoubtedly interesting, he was not a man I would previously have felt to be deserving in any way of my help in being heard, but things had changed.

Not that I can claim I immediately spotted this opportunity when destiny first came knocking. When the first call came out of the blue I was even a little impatient with the evasions of the softly spoken man on the other end of the telephone, who merely introduced himself as being "from the embassy".

"My minister would like to meet you," he told me. "He is going to be in Zurich tomorrow."

"Who is your minister?" I asked, intrigued despite myself.

"He would very much like to meet you," he continued as if I hadn't spoken. "A flight has been booked for you and we can arrange for a car to take you to and from the airports."

It really had been as simple and as vague as that. However much I mumbled my doubts at whether I could spare the time, the man from the embassy was quietly insistent. It did not seem to occur to him that non compliance with his "minister's" request was even a possibility. I found myself worn down with the quiet determination and reasonable tone of his voice. The next day a Mercedes arrived at the house and took me to the airport where I found the business class booking had been made in my name just as he promised, and I was "fast tracked" through to the plane, feeling simultaneously smug and self-conscious as I walked past those who were patiently queuing. Another car was waiting for me at Zurich Airport and the driver took me directly to the hotel. The whole journey had been as effortless for me as a trip to the local shops. No wonder the rich always look so unruffled by the trying logistics of life that leave most of us drained by the end of every day.

The man from the embassy was there ahead of me, waiting in the foyer to present me to his boss like some sort of trophy. He was younger than I had imagined from our telephone conversation and so immaculate in his appearance that for a moment I mistook him for part of the hotel management team. The Minister was waiting on a sofa beside a blazing log fire, coffee and biscuits, bottles of water and crystal glasses spread out on the table in front of him, dressed in cashmere and loafers, as if he were welcoming me to his own home. His smile was broad and his arms spread wide across the back of the sofa, making him look far bigger than he actually was when he stood up to greet me. As we talked, a series of children and teenagers came and went from his presence and I realised that he was travelling with his whole family, effortlessly fitting business and pleasure together on the same expense account.

"We have a lot in common," he beamed at me. "I am a writer too. I edited an important newspaper for many years and I used to write my own opinion pieces. One day I will write a great book about everything that I have seen and everything that I know."

At no stage of the meeting did anyone explain clearly why I was there, although by the end I had grasped the fact that his job title was something like Minister of Information and that he had been deputed to find a ghostwriter for someone of even more importance than him. I worked out who this person was without being told. I had a faint idea that he was generally viewed as an authoritarian ruler, but one who had been tolerated by the rest of the world for a very long time for a variety of reasons, the main one being the large amounts of oil and other minerals stored under his country. I felt stirrings of unease at the thought of assisting such a person in any way, but at the same time they had succeeded in piquing my curiosity as skilfully as any film director or thriller writer might, and of course there was the lure of the surreal fee. The Minister gave no indication that he had any knowledge of anything I might have written in the past, but the man from the embassy accompanied me back to the airport in the Mercedes after the meeting and opened up a little.

"You have a reputation for being a man of great integrity," he said, "and for writing books of great truth and honesty. Those are the qualities that we want this book to demonstrate."

"No they fucking aren't," Caroline said when I relayed the comment to her that night in bed, trying to sound self-deprecating and cynical at the same time. "They want the credibility that your past books will give to their shoddy little public relations exercise. They will lie to you from start to finish and you will be obliged to pass on those lies to the world with your stamp of approval."

I knew she was right but I still felt crestfallen to have my balloon of self-importance punctured so rudely after a long day of being flattered and pampered.

"But it is a lot of money," I said eventually, "and we really do need a lot of money."

She didn't respond, merely turning over and feigning sleep, as she had done every night since the afternoon when everything changed.

I don't think I would have recognised the minister the next time we met, had I not been briefed that he would be there at the first meeting to introduce me personally to Mo or rather, "His Excellency". The confident, casually dressed man holding court in a five star Zurich hotel lounge had been replaced by a humble palace lackey in a two piece suit and discreet tie. All his body language conveyed humility and respect in the presence of his leader, the man to whom he no doubt owed his entire five-star lifestyle. He kept shooting me anxious looks, seemingly worried that I was not showing the correct level of deference. I had never been in the presence of a world leader before and had no idea what that correct level might be, so I was relying on simply being pleasant and polite, in the manner I had been taught as a child. Mo seemed perfectly happy with whatever it was I was doing and talked all the way through the meeting as if the decision to hire me had already been made. After the meeting, once the minister had re-inflated himself, he informed me that they were going to be talking to several other writers before they made a final decision, but I was pretty sure he was lying. Since money was the main reason I was going to accept the job, I did not intend to fall for any negotiating tactics and merely assured him that I would wait to hear.

In the end they didn't even try to haggle, simply accepting my price and agreeing to pay half in advance. I immediately regretted not asking for more but I had never been in a world where the sort of money I was talking about is of absolutely of no importance to those who are paying, so I had no way of gauging anything. I was as lost as Alice in Wonderland but that actually added to the excitement of the adventure. Their only concern seemed to be that I should sign a legally-binding confidentiality agreement. I was summoned to lawyers' offices in one of the tallest and glassiest of modern towers in the City of London, peopled by the smoothest-looking men and women I had ever seen outside the Hollywood movies. Three of them, two men and a woman, were waiting for me in an office big enough to be a boardroom. From their heavy fountain pens to the shine of the table where the papers were spread out for me to sign, there was an intimidating – but at the same time reassuring – reek of power and money in the air. I felt simultaneously protected and threatened, empowered and overwhelmed.

They didn't seem to be in any hurry to conclude the business. I guess they were all billing by the hour and they seemed genuinely interested in finding out about my role in the proceedings. The leader of the meeting was a grey-haired man in his fifties, sleek and tanned in an utterly uncreased blue suit, white shirt and red tie. He seemed puzzled and intrigued by the whole idea of ghostwriting.

"Do you think you can provide what our client needs?" he asked once I had explained a little of how the process usually worked.

"Provided he gives me the material I need to work with."

"You will need to work fast," the other man in the meeting said with a smirk and they all smiled as if they were in on a private joke which they had no intention of sharing with me.

"I can work fast."

"So we understand."

"So you already know something about me," I said, feeling that for just a second I had won an advantage in whatever game it was we were playing.

"We did some research," the woman said. She seemed the most hostile of the three of them, as if she suspected me of harbouring some nefarious ulterior motive for taking the job. "It wasn't hard. You are well documented on the internet for someone whose work is supposed to be so secret."

"Only some of it becomes public knowledge," I said, annoyed to find myself feeling defensive again. It was as if she was accusing me of being a self-publicist. "With many of my projects no one apart from the client knows I have any connection to the eventual book at all. Even Google doesn't know everything."

Once the papers had been signed, and once they felt confident that I understood the ferocity with which they would come after me if I did anything that remotely contravened the conditions I had just signed up to, I was escorted graciously and firmly from the building. My electronic visitor's pass was deactivated and lifted from round my neck by a security guard who was careful to make no eye contact.

When the first payment arrived in my humble current account, my bank must have thought there had been some sort of mistake – or maybe they suspected me of money laundering – because someone contacted me directly, which had never happened before, and asked if I would like him to come to the house so we could discuss places I could invest the money. I declined politely because Caroline and I both knew what we were going to have to do with every penny of it.

If things had been different Caroline would have told me exactly what she thought of me for selling my soul in such a shameful way and I would almost certainly have declined the job as a result. I might have felt a glimmer of disappointment not to be spending more time wandering around Wonderland, but I would have been relieved at the same time to have been reminded of where the right path in life lay. One of the reasons I love her as deeply as I do is because I respect her judgement in all matters of morality and ethics. We both share the same ideals but there had been other occasions where I had allowed myself to be seduced by some charismatic sinner and to temporarily lose my moral perspective. Whenever that happened I could always rely on Caroline to turn the lights back on for me with a few choice words or even just a look of incredulity at my credulity. But now things were different. Because of what I had caused to happen to us she had to accept that we needed the money too much to be able to be too scrupulous about who or where it was coming from. I could tell that she hated me even more for forcing her to compromise her principles than for being willing to compromise my own, so we never mentioned the matter again, making the silences between us even longer and more painful. There were now so many subjects that we could no longer bear to talk about.

8

"I found some photographs for you to look at," Lou said, beckoning me in through the open kitchen door. I had made my own way over to his house uninvited, feeling confident that I would receive a welcome and being eager to escape the palace.

Coming out of my bedroom that morning I had actually let out a small but foolish scream on coming face to face with a fully armed soldier standing amongst the fresh flower arrangements in the plushly carpeted and curtained corridor. On closer inspection, I realised that he was little more than a boy despite all his padding and the intimidating, complex-looking gun that he was clutching to his chest in readiness for action. He seemed almost as surprised to see me as I was to see him but he regained his self control faster than I did and raised a calming hand to reassure me that he was there for my protection. I said something banal, self conscious and jokey, which he obviously didn't understand but he grinned politely anyway.

By the time I had reached the office wing I had passed at least a dozen more like him, each of them posted at a strategic position to be able to cover a door or a window that might be used as an entrance by attackers. Mo was locked down in a meeting with more soldiers on the doors and although I made sure my phone was switched on in readiness I held out little hope of being able to get any time with him today.

Lou was on his own at the kitchen table, flicking through a pile of photograph albums with what looked like genuine excitement. "Here," he said, "sit."

I sat beside him, took an album and began to turn pages.

"So many memories," he sighed. "So many things that I have forgotten in my life. It is like looking at another young man, nothing to do with me."

In my head I had pictured a complete hippy when he had talked about their times together in the Sixties, but the pictures showed two fairly conventional young men. Their hair might have been a little longer than their parents would have approved of but they still looked like well groomed, wealthy, young playboys – more St Tropez in open topped sports cars than San Francisco in psychedelic camper vans. They both wore expensive sun glasses, white trousers and white polo shirts tight enough to show off torsos they were obviously proud of, more Gucci than Grandma's Attic. They did have discreet beads around their necks and wrists but certainly no flowers in their hair.

"You were both very good looking," I said.

"Youth always looks good from this distance don't you think?" he laughed, apparently pleased with the compliment. "Not that you are looking from as many years away as I am. We were both very self confident, which is the greatest secret of success when you are young, don't you think? You have no wisdom or experience to draw on but you don't care because you think it is all old fashioned bullshit anyway. If you can just give your children self confidence they can ask for no more."

I felt a stab of pain at the thought of the terrible endowment I had given to Becky and forced myself to concentrate on the pictures.

"Ah," he exclaimed with genuine pleasure, "look at how beautiful Claudia was!" He opened an album that was somewhat larger than the others as reverentially as if it contained some fragile and valuable ancient scriptures and showed me two front covers from two different international editions of *Vogue*, Claudia was on both of them.

"Claudia is a model?"

"Not now," he laughed, "not with the children to look after, but she modelled for a few years before. She liked to have a little money of her own. I encouraged it because I think if someone is beautiful they should be allowed to celebrate it while it lasts. She will always have these pictures to look back on," he lowered his voice conspiratorially, "even when she is old and looks like Sanka!" He gave one of his deepest laughs. "Also it gave her many happy memories of being the centre of attention. She deserved that after all she had gone through as a child."

Another album was full of pictures of Lou back in Italy with his family. "Is this your family home?" I asked, tilting the album for him to see. "It's stunning."

"Yes. It was built as a summer house for one of the Popes six or seven hundred years ago and the following generations have improved and extended it. It is very beautiful. You can see why I did not want the family to lose it."

"You are descended from a Pope?"

He shrugged. "Nearly everyone in Italy can trace their family back to someone high in the Church sooner or later. We have our fair share."

He seemed to be rediscovering the pictures at the same time as I was discovering them, exclaiming and laughing with each new revelation. "Look at this!" "Oh, this brings back memories!" "My God, I had forgotten that!"

In the later photographs of the two young men together they had only changed a little, but the settings of the pictures had become very different. Everyone around them was always wearing suits and ties if they weren't in military uniforms and there didn't seem to be many women in any of the group photographs. There were endless pictures of men lining up to shake hands with one another and posing for trophy pictures on the sealing of some deal or other. Occasionally there were more candid photographs taken during formal-looking banquets or while one or other of them, usually Mo, was on a podium giving a speech. There were pictures from all over the world: from Britain to China, Washington to Moscow, often with recognisable world leaders and many at huge factories or on airfields or on podiums watching soldiers parading past.

"Why are you showing him those? Are you stupid?" Claudia's voice made me jump, partly because my nerves were already on edge, partly because I hadn't heard her come in and partly because I hadn't imagined her capable of such sharpness of tone.

"It's just pictures," Lou said, apparently unbothered by her obvious anger.

"If Mo wanted him to see pictures he would have said so. Has he said anything?"

"Why would Mo care? He is telling our friend here all his secrets."

"No more pictures," she said, firmly closing the albums and packing them away. Lou raised his hands in surrender and winked at me as she lugged them out of the room.

"It was his job then," she said to me when she returned, her voice still angry. "That was then and not now. Now he is a gardener and a good man. A good husband and a good father."

I nodded, unable to gauge what reaction she expected of me, not sure why she was saying these things.

"Claudia," he stood up and took her in his arms as if to calm her. "It's okay. He is a friend. He is on our side. It is good that he understands a little more."

I was flattered that he described me as a friend, but still confused by what had just happened. I was trying to imagine why she should be so anxious to brush her husband's past under the carpet. Was she jealous of a time when she didn't know him, or was there something to be hidden, to be ashamed of? And if I was their friend, did that mean I was also their co-conspirator in some way? I felt slightly sick at the possibilities that such a connection might raise. What exactly had all those men in suits and uniforms been doing in the photographs that Claudia obviously wanted to ensure did not get included in anything I might write?

9

"Hello, you won't know me, my name is Caroline Springer."

Those were the first words that I ever heard pass Caroline's lips when I received her call from out of the blue. Her accent was American and her voice sounded light and playful, someone you instantly wanted to hear more from.

"I am an editor," she went on, "with a publisher called Petteridge. You probably won't have heard of us."

I had actually heard of them because most of my life was spent scouring lists of publishers trying to work out who to send manuscripts and proposals to, but I didn't say anything because I thought it might sound as if I was just trying to flatter her.

"Do you still do ghostwriting?"

"Very much so."

"Only I have a project that I think might be up your street. We can't pay very much up front but we think it has great possibilities."

At that stage I would have accepted virtually any assignment from any publisher, just to improve my C.V., but she wasn't to know that. If a project then made money that was a bonus and if it turned out to be interesting and worthwhile even better. None of this did I tell her, of course, I merely listened as she gave me a rough outline of the story. A manuscript had arrived on her desk from a man who had been part of a plot to assassinate General Pinochet in Chile. He had spent time as a political prisoner and had suffered terrible torture at the hands of the authorities.

"It's an incredible story," Caroline enthused, "but English is not his first language and I don't think he has a great deal of education. He needs a lot of help. Would you be interested in meeting him?"

Not only was I very interested in meeting him, I was also interested in meeting her. The more publishers and editors I got to know, the better my chances of getting other assignments and of selling other projects that I was already working on. We made a date for me to go in to the Petteridge offices in Notting Hill, which turned out to be in the rather grand and well-worn private house of Arnold Petteridge, the company's founder and owner. I can still picture exactly what I was expecting Caroline to look like before I met her. I had expected her to be in her forties or fifties, not particularly interested in her personal appearance but intensely interested in the sort of social and political causes that Petteridge was known for publishing books on. I guess that picture stays with me as clearly as it does because of the shock I felt when she came down to the front hall which doubled as a reception area and where I was sitting waiting in a dilapidated leather wing chair.

It sounds like a writer's cliché to say that she took my breath away, but it is a precise and accurate description of what happened. I literally struggled to gurgle anything intelligible as

I shook her hand and stared at her perfect little face like a slack jawed idiot. She was, and still is more than twenty years later, an exquisitely beautiful woman. It's not just me saying that because I am in love with her, every man she even passes a few moments with is reduced to bumbling foolishness by her perfection. She is simply the wisest, kindest and most beautiful creature I have ever met. I'm sure she must have had the same effect on Arnold Petteridge when she first breezed in for a job interview. She later told me that she fell a little in love with Petteridge herself that day, seeing everything romantic that she had come to London to find contained in the fusty, book-lined rooms of the house that had been in his family for many generations.

"It felt like I had stepped out of the modern world and straight into the pages of a Dickens novel," she said. "I knew it was the world I wanted to stay in forever – a bit like Harry Potter arriving at Hogwarts for the first time, going through into another dimension."

The Chilean revolutionary was already sitting in the chaotic little office that Caroline shared with two other editors somewhere up in the eaves of the house. He looked like Che Guevara as he appeared on the famous posters, all the way to his carefully trimmed face hair. The intensity of his stare was unnerving as Caroline brought me in and introduced us. He held onto my hand with his strong bony fingers long after I had started to feel uncomfortable. Caroline had organised for us to have sandwiches while we talked but none of us remembered to eat as we listened, mesmerised. We sat in virtually silent awe as he regaled us with his tales of revolutionary life in the jungles of Chile and the horrors of the prisons and government torture chambers. He showed us vivid scars, exposing private parts of his body without hesitation. I guess when you have been subjected to the ultimate debasement showing your body to a room full of pretty young editors is not too challenging. All the time I was listening to him I was fighting the urge to turn and stare at Caroline's profile. Her cheek was so close to mine in the cramped conditions of the office I believed I could feel the heat from her skin, although it might have been my own blushes I was sensing.

High on several different kinds of excitement I remember walking back to the bus stop after the meeting thinking that if I couldn't marry Caroline I would never ever be able to find anyone else who would match her perfection. The excitement was quickly followed by panic and then despair at the prospect of possibly failing to win her and never again being happy. I guess everyone feels like that when they fall deeply and instantly in love and in most cases the feeling wears off with time, but for me it never has, despite everything that we have been through together. Even now, when she has drifted so far away from me in every sense of the phrase, I cannot even think about her without feeling tearful.

I agreed to write the book – as I'm sure she knew I would – and I invited her out for a date the next day, which she later confessed she had also known I would. The date went incredibly well and we were pretty much living together within a month. The book was an enormous success, allowing us to spend even more time together and Caroline agreed to marry me a couple of years later. I felt that Destiny was looking after me and that feeling gave me the confidence to keep going as a writer, however hard it might be to make a living wage. That confidence also made me careless and absent minded about practical things that deserved more attention, but Caroline was always there to remember arrangements I might have forgotten and to tidy up any messes that I left in my wake.

"It's okay," she would say every time I apologised for something new, "you concentrate on the writing, I'll take care of the rest." It made her the perfect editor for me and also the perfect wife.

The success of the book brought other people with similar stories to Petteridge's door and often, if they were not able to undertake the writing themselves, they would ask to have me as their ghostwriter. I nearly always agreed if Caroline or Arnold asked me, although none of the subsequent books enjoyed the same level of sales as that first one. Arnold must have made a lot of money from that Chilean story but he had soon spent it on advances for other causes which he deemed equally worthy. As readership of the first book spread out around the world via many skilful translations, people also came forward to claim that the story the author had told was not exactly the whole story. Some even accused him of lying, or of fabricating. One or two said that they had been in prisons that he mentioned or partaken in skirmishes which he had described first hand, and they had never come across him. It was always disturbing to receive letters or emails from such people, but they were few and far between compared to the numbers who wrote saying how much they admired the author, how much they loved the book, how inspired they had been by his courage and how much they had learned from his experiences. I have lost count over the years of the number of people who have told me it is their favourite book ever. Some of the doubting voices were obviously lacking in credibility, others were able to tell their stories just as convincingly as the author himself.

Caroline and I shared many moments of doubt when someone new emerged to tell a different story, but whenever we confronted the author with whatever the new evidence might be he was always able to put our minds at rest. Eventually I came to the conclusion that there are as many sides to any story as there are witnesses who wish to talk about it. Often no one is lying, they are merely telling what they know and what they believe. I began to doubt whether there was any such thing as an objective truth, concluding that everything was subjective. That led me to believe that everyone should be given a chance to tell their side of any story and that time would then tell which versions proved the most popular or the most credible. Here, in Mo's palace, that belief was being stretched agonisingly close to breaking point.

10

"Please forgive Claudia her outburst," Lou said when I next saw him. "She comes from a country where retribution is a way of life. People can bear a grudge for generations. It makes her wary of everyone and everything. I think perhaps she spends too much time with her mother. Sanka is full of hatred and fear."

"That is not surprising," I said.

"I know. Still I wish Claudia could find a more complete peace in her heart but I fear the damage is too deep to ever be completely healed now."

"I understand that sort of damage."

"Do you?"

"Yes."

He watched me for a moment to see if I was going to say any more, but I didn't. Nor did he attempt to explain any more about Claudia's experiences as we sat in a Chinese pavilion beside some fish ponds and listened to the gunfire on the other side of the walls.

"Mo is coming to the house for some supper tonight," he said eventually. "Why don't you come too?"

"That would be great."

I was surprised. I'm not even sure I believed him. Would Mo really have the time to go out for supper considering everything that was happening? Lou made it sound so casual and matter of fact.

"Even great dictators have to eat you know," he said and I saw that he had guessed my thoughts and was mocking my doubts.

"I guess so."

"Come first so that you are there when he arrives, then it will seem more natural that you stay on."

"Okay."

"It will be interesting for you to see him in less formal surroundings, to see him amongst old friends."

"It certainly will."

A few hours later I was sitting in the kitchen watching Claudia and Sanka cooking. Claudia made no reference to her outburst regarding the photographs beyond giving my hand a reassuring squeeze as she pecked me on the cheek. It reminded me of how it had felt when Caroline used to show me little signs of affection at unexpected moments and it brought long suppressed tears to the surface.

"I'm sorry," she said as she saw me wipe my eyes, "my mother has been chopping so many onions, I think I must stink from them."

I didn't correct her because I wouldn't have known how to begin explaining how such a light touch from her finger tips could elicit so violent a reaction. There was such a lack of formality in their preparation of the meal I wondered if there had been a change of plan but an hour or so later Mo arrived, completely alone and unguarded, and carrying a wooden box which he dropped on the table so that his hands were free to hug and kiss Lou and the two women and to shake my hand as if he wasn't remotely surprised to find me there. I guessed someone in his intelligence service had informed him. I knew there were cameras all round the grounds so they would have known my movements.

"A gift from Tony Blair!" he laughed, gesturing at the box. "I think perhaps this would be a good time to drink it, no?"

Lou opened the box and reverentially lifted out one of the bottles to examine it under the light. "Château Lafite," he said approvingly. "I most certainly think we should drink a toast to poor Tony with that."

While Lou opened a couple of the bottles, which must have been worth close to a thousand pounds each, and Mo flirted with Sanka who giggled like a schoolgirl, it felt almost like one of the hundreds of kitchen dinner parties that Caroline and I must have been to together over the years in London, albeit bearing less expensive gifts.

"Remember this, Mo?" Lou asked, dropping a photograph down beside Mo's glass of wine. "I found it while I was showing my albums to our friend here."

I glanced across at Claudia, wondering if she would erupt again, but she didn't seem to be listening as she worked. Mo pulled out a pair of half-moon, tortoiseshell rimmed reading glasses, something I had never seen him do before, and picked up the picture to study it. "Ah, yes, yes, yes," he smiled at the memories it evoked. "Studio 54 in New York, no?"

"Yes. And see who is there beside you?"

Mo peered more closely and then burst out laughing. "Yes, yes, Bianca. Bianca Jagger. Wonderful, wonderful."

"She was celebrating her divorce then I think."

"Yes, I think so. I think so." Mo turned to me. "Do you know Bianca?"

"I was introduced to her once," I said. "She had an involvement with someone I wrote a book for, or at least they had an involvement in the same cause."

"Such an interesting woman," Mo said, taking a gulp of his wine. "Very interesting woman. A great fighter for human rights. Many, many good causes."

"And a good dancer too," Lou prompted him.

"Yes," Mo brightened again at this fresh memory. "A very, very good dancer."

Claudia looked up and tutted in mock disapproval of their foolish men talk and they both laughed.

"I have to tell you, my young friend," Mo slapped me on the shoulder, "that Claudia here is also a very good dancer."

Claudia took an olive stone from her mouth and flicked it at him. It bounced off the side of his head, making him laugh even more uproariously and drain his glass dry, holding it out for Mo to refill.

"Why don't you come to Italy with us, Mo?" Lou said as he poured, suddenly serious. "Before it is too late. Zana and the girls are already in Milan."

"Ah," Mo sighed, "yes, the great shopping expedition."

"You could stay in my mother's old room. You remember the view from that room?"

"Yes, of course I remember," Mo said, his laughter subsiding and his expression becoming slightly dreamy, perhaps from the wine or perhaps from the memory. "But there are still things to do here before I can take a holiday. Once I leave there will be chaos. There is no one to take over, just a mob. When my father died I promised to serve the people and they need me now more than ever. I cannot run away from them just because a few troublemakers are shouting in the streets."

"They are no longer just a few," Lou said and I saw a spark

of anger flash in Mo's eyes, like he was about to challenge his old friend to a fight.

"Stupid!" he barked. "They are so stupid. Don't these idiots realise how this will make our country look to the world? To the financial markets? The financial people do not like to see civil unrest. The Chinese won't like it. After all the work we have done to bring money into this country. The people have never been so rich or so secure. They complain about traffic jams but do you think they had cars in my father's day? He kept them in donkey carts. Is that what they would prefer to go back to?"

"You are a misunderstood man, my friend," Lou said.

"Such plans we have for the future. The developments, the tourists, the new airport, so many things, but they will all go if our friends in other countries change their minds about investing. Why don't they help us?"

"Who?" Lou asked.

"The international community. Why don't they send in peacekeepers to disperse the crowds? All they do is whisper to me that I should leave, but if I go there will be far more chaos I tell you."

"They think that if they help you they will have to help all the others."

"But the others are different!"

"We are all the same to them."

"Ah, go back to pruning your roses, old man. Leave the politics to me."

"Just don't leave it too late, Mo," Lou said as Sanka served up steaming bowls of lamb stew and Claudia produced some freshly baked bread from the oven. "Really, I mean it. If you go now maybe you will be able to return once things have settled down and they can see that the alternative is worse. If you stay too long there will be no possibility of coming back, perhaps you won't even be able to leave alive."

"Oh, Lou," Mo laughed and raised his glass, "drink the wine and enjoy life while you have it." Lou reluctantly returned the salute and both men drained their glasses. Mo suddenly seemed to remember that I was there. "So, Mr Ghostwriter, sitting there with your ears and eyes taking in everything. What do you make of it all?"

"I'm just here to make a book," I said and concentrated on eating.

11

Arnold Petteridge knew exactly what a treasure he had in Caroline and when he heard that we were looking for somewhere to start our married life together he suggested that we rented his basement flat at about half the market price. We wouldn't have been able to afford to live in Notting Hill on what we were earning any other way – despite the success of the Chilean book – and we ended up staying there for ten years, partly because we were so completely happy neither of us wanted to do anything that might break the spell. Notting Hill was transforming from being a slightly run down, bohemian part of town to being one of the most fashionable and sought after areas in the city. That made it an exciting place to live, even though we had no financial stake in the rising property values, which made us a mystery to virtually everyone we met. No one could understand why we didn't want to "get a foot on the property ladder", but nothing we could afford would have been as magical as living in Arnold's basement with its French doors out to the secluded garden, rendered silent by the walls of mighty houses standing between us and the roar of the busier streets. We ate most of our meals out there on a scrappy bit of lawn during the summer, shaded by almost rotted, wooden trellis-work held up by knotted stems of ancient climbers. During the winter we retreated into the large, warm kitchen that had originally served the whole house. Every spring the cherry trees that lined the street outside our front door burst into pink blossom which cascaded down past our windows at the first hint of a breeze. Some days it felt like Mary Poppins must be hovering just above our rooftops.

Arnold cooked for himself in a kitchenette that had been installed upstairs during the Sixties, when he had first started to subdivide the property and hire people to work for him, remaining cheerfully self-sufficient even as his physical strength began to fade and his gangling frame withered.

Eventually Arnold died and his family wanted to sell the gently rotting but now enormously valuable house. The business had been struggling to make a profit for some years, mainly due to Arnold's habit of giving large sums of money to the causes that he published books about, and so it seemed a propitious moment for Caroline and I to re-think what we were going to do with our lives next. Caroline had an English aunt who owned a dilapidated woodman's cottage in the country outside London and she asked us if we would like to have it. It needed almost total re-building but we had managed to save a little money by then and I had been earning for long enough to be able to get a small mortgage as well, despite being freelance. Much of the restoration work, however, we were going to have to learn how to do ourselves. I bought myself a second hand tool kit from the local market on the first weekend after we moved in. I was filled with optimism at the many new skills I was sure I was about to master.

We left London with a few regrets but very quickly became

absorbed in creating our new home. Caroline continued to do some freelance editing at one end of the kitchen table while I wrote at the other. The blossoming of our latent nesting instincts was followed by the joyful discovery that Caroline had fallen pregnant. It seemed as if our lives were charmed, as if everything always fell into place for us and always would. I'm not saying we didn't have the normal ups and downs of any young married couple on low incomes, but had a genie popped up with the usual three wishes, neither of us would have changed anything about our existence together during those wonderful years.

When Becky was born she was a dream baby, giving us none of the challenges that many of our new baby-owning friends seemed to be going through. No colic, no tantrums, lots of gurgles and smiles and long nights of blissfully undisturbed sleep. The cottage grew more and more idyllic under our loving stewardship and the garden acquired a chicken coop and a pen for a couple of goats, two of my earliest attempts at construction work, and a vegetable garden, also penned in to protect it from the rabbits, and from the goats and chickens when they escaped from their own designated compounds.

I had never felt the urge to do any gardening in London, beyond trimming back so we had enough space to sit and eat or read. Maybe it has something to do with ownership, or perhaps having another generation to improve things for makes a difference, because suddenly I wanted to be out there all the time. The grounds had been as rampantly overgrown as the house had been dilapidated, but underneath the years of neglect there lurked a traditional English garden of the sort that might have featured on the lid of an olde worlde tin of English biscuits. I started by clearing a space for Becky to be able to play safely and that small act soon grew into a sort of obsession as I spread my efforts wider and wider. Because the garden had hardly been touched for thirty years, it had none of the imported plants which had become fashionable during that time and I became obsessed by the idea of only ever planting things that were indigenous to England. Caroline used to become quite frustrated sometimes when she would see something wonderful in a garden centre and I would refuse to buy it because it wasn't traditionally English.

"You know what you are?" she would say.

"Yes," I would reply, because she said it so often, "a garden fascist!"

"We shall have racial purity in the borders," she would declare in a cod Nazi accent, sometimes even adding a little Nazi salute.

There were times when she would smuggle some foreign born plant in without telling me, or would invent some totally specious provenance for something she had purchased on a whim.

"There are references to these in Chaucer," she would tell me with an utterly straight face. "I swear to God, they are as English as Churchill."

"His mother was American."

"Loser!"

I thought about taking photographs of the palace garden with all its serried ranks of trees standing to attention, its triumphal statuary and the immaculate topiary that Lou and his teams spent their days clipping to smooth perfection, and emailing them to her with some covering note like "so you think I'm a garden Fascist!", but I could no longer be sure that she would laugh and it would sound like a feeble, trivial, self-regarding joke.

Within six or seven years the cottage was exactly the sort of home I had always imagined happy families to live in, it was the stuff of early twentieth century children's stories. There were dogs and cats, puppies and kittens and Becky grew strong and clever and pretty and happy. Maybe I wasn't grateful enough for what we had. Maybe I got a bit smug, (Lou might applaud it as "self-confidence", I suppose). Maybe I assumed this was just the way life panned out if you did pretty much all the good and right things.

12

There seemed to be even more chaos and panic when I woke the following morning and went out into the garden to see why there was a JCB digger at work on one of Lou's lawns. I had spotted it from my bedroom window, but it was invisible from ground level behind the high, thick hedges when I came outside; all the chaos contained and disguised.

In one of our early conversations Lou had talked about a sixteenth century Chinese philosopher called Ji Cheng. "Ji Cheng believed that it was a garden designer's job to hide the vulgar and the common as far as the eye can see," he had said, "and include only the excellent and splendid. He taught that garden design was all about concealment and surprise. A garden is not meant to be seen all at once, but should be laid out to present a series of scenes."

"Concealment and surprise" had sounded such a delightful phrase, but now, as I looked at the apparently tranquil garden in front of me, it gave me a sick feeling of foreboding deep in my stomach, without my being able to understand why that might be.

If there hadn't been such an air of confusion everywhere inside the palace that day I doubt if I would have been able to just stroll through the gap in the hedges and witness the scene going on inside that particular enclosure. Someone should have been watching my progress on a screen and there should have been a guard placed on the outside to discourage anyone from approaching but there was not. In fact it took several minutes for one of the guards to see me there and hurry over to escort me back out through the hedge and shoo me away. It was just luck that he didn't shoot me on sight because no one else working on that lawn would have cared.

In those minutes, during which I stood and stared and failed to comprehend anything clearly, I was able to see a number of things. I was able to see that the JCB had dug a deep, neat trench and that the driver was now lounging in the cab, smoking a cigarette and waiting to be given his next instruction. I assume now that that instruction was going to be to fill in the trench again once it had served its purpose, but I had no way of knowing that during those shocking minutes. I saw soldiers, some of whom I recognised from their guard duties around the palace, working silently in pairs to throw naked men's bodies into the trench. Most of the bodies had their hands tied behind their backs and some also had their ankles tied together. Most of them had a great many ugly welts and bruises on their bodies and all of them had bullet holes in the backs of their heads and parts of their faces had been blown away. I didn't have the presence of mind to count them and I couldn't see how many were already at the bottom of the trench. I don't think my mind was working in anything like a logical manner, being overwhelmed by a mixture of unfamiliar emotions, but thinking back now I suspect there were at least twenty bodies in and around that trench, perhaps as many as thirty.

Once I had been ejected from the gruesome, leafy enclosure by a guard who seemed in two minds as to whether he should add me to the pile of corpses, I walked across to Lou's house in a trance, unsure whether or not I was going to throw up. Part of me wanted to inform him of this terrible thing that was happening to his sacred garden, but another part of me was already beginning to question if I had actually seen what I thought I had. I was questioning my own sanity. I suppose it was simply too much for me to take in, too different from any experience I had ever had.

I don't actually remember that walk, but I do remember standing at the kitchen door looking in and seeing Claudia bent over the open lid of the stove, feeding photographs into the hungry flames below, her face flushed from the heat. She didn't look surprised to see me and didn't stop what she was doing.

"He is just an old man working in the gardens. That is all they need to see if they come here," she said. "Just a harmless gardener."

Sanka was sitting in the corner of the room, bent double with her face in her hands, her shoulders heaving with sobs. It sounded like she was praying. Beside her were several bags which looked as if they contained all her worldly goods, as if she was prepared to go somewhere at a moment's notice. The bags looked as if they had been used for such a purpose many times in the past, their corners battered and scarred, worn away with difficult travel. She had a scarf tied round her hair and the girls were standing each side of her, both touching her as if to console her but staring silently around them, their eyes wide with anxiety as their mother worked feverishly over the stove.

"Where is Lou?" I asked.

"With Mo in the palace."

She gave no sign that she wanted me to stay or that she

intended to offer me any hospitality and Sanka did not raise her head from her hands or stop her incantations, so I walked back up to the palace by another route, avoiding the area where I thought I had witnessed the mass grave diggers at work. I noticed that I was having difficulty breathing regularly and worried that I might faint from lack of oxygen.

13

One of the things that I have noticed about families – well, about people in general really – is how similar we all are in many ways. Caroline and I knew a number of other young couples having their first children at the same as us and we all conformed to the same stereotypes in many ways. Us men all thought we wanted to do much more with things like nappies and night feeds than we ever actually did, for instance. We all thought our own children were more clever and beautiful than everyone else's, which simply wasn't possible when you stopped to think about it. As soon as the babies grew into adventurous toddlers their fathers would encourage them to ever greater feats of daring and experimentation, while the mothers would try to dissuade them from taking unnecessary risks and would become infuriated with the fathers who they saw as being careless with the lives of their precious offspring.

"You can't keep him/her wrapped in cotton wool forever," the fathers would say.

"For God's sake take some responsibility for what happens

to your child," the women would wail as they dealt with another bumped head or grazed knee.

Caroline and I were no different to everyone else in these respects, although we liked to think we were. Like many of the other men I knew, however, I was also completely convinced that my wife was the most marvellous mother in the world, even if she did sometimes fuss too much over a scrape or a sting collected during a father-daughter crawl through the undergrowth, or a grubby, sticky sweet that might get picked up off the floor and popped straight back into an eager mouth.

Becky and I spent a great deal of time together as she grew bigger and ever more talkative. Although most of the crucial work on the house was completed, I had caught the home and garden improvement bugs by that stage and I spent a huge part of my life when I wasn't writing pottering around building things, chopping things or digging things. I wasn't particularly skilful at any of it, and I could often see Caroline trying to stifle a giggle at some of the bodging that I would proudly present to her at the end of the day. She would nearly always end up suggesting that we call in a professional to "finish the job off properly" for me, but the overall effects of my labours were satisfying enough for me to keep going despite my shortcomings.

Becky was totally fascinated by everything I did and shared none of her mother's misgivings about her father's brilliance as a craftsman. She always wanted to be doing whatever it was with me. I can't pretend there weren't moments when I couldn't have progressed faster without her assistance, but overall I knew that I was fortunate to have such an opportunity to spend time with my daughter, listening to her chatter, building a relationship at the same time as teaching her a few basic life skills. Many of my male friends would complain about the tedium of having to spend hours playing childish games that made them want to scream with boredom but I never felt like that. If I had a job I particularly wanted to finish or which I thought might prove too dangerous for small fingers and wide eyes, I would make sure I did it while she was at school or visiting a friend. I realise now that those were supremely glorious years for all three of us.

Despite her misgivings, Caroline was always very encouraging to both of us in all our endeavours, although I think she might have liked it if Becky had showed a little more interest in helping her to prepare meals or in reading books with her, which were the two greatest loves in Caroline's life apart from us. And there were times when she would be horrified by the tools that I would allow Becky to handle, anticipating all sorts of dreadful accidents that never happened because I always tried to teach Becky the basic safety precautions and because she was a particularly adept and well co-ordinated child.

There were one or two books with which Caroline did manage to catch Becky's attention. One was *The Secret Garden*, which told a story of finding a mysterious overgrown garden hidden behind walls, which Becky could relate directly to the work she and I did together in the garden. The other was a picture book version of *Tarzan of the Apes*, which had some particularly silly illustrations of the tree house where Tarzan and Jane set up home together. Becky was completely entranced with the idea of building a house in a tree and talked about it endlessly.

There were several very large trees in the garden and she would spend hours wandering around them and climbing up those which had accessible lower branches, trying to persuade me that we should build a tree house together.

"Maybe I should build one for her birthday," I suggested to

Caroline one evening after Becky was asleep and we were sitting together in the garden with a bottle of wine.

"You?" she said with genuine shock which then turned to laughter. "Sorry, but aren't they quite difficult to build?"

"Harsh!" I teased. "I think she would rather we built it ourselves. I think that would be part of the fun for her. If we get one 'off the shelf' it won't have the same sentimental value. Imagine her being able to show her children and tell them she built it with her Dad."

"You don't have to buy anything off the shelf," she persisted. "You and Becky could design it together and then get a carpenter to put it up."

"Have you any idea what a carpenter would cost? And that would be on top of the cost of the timber and everything else. I'm sure we can do it."

"I think it's a lovely idea," she said, squeezing my hand, "but I'm really not happy about the two of you clambering around ten feet off the ground with saws and hammers and God knows what else. She is only a little girl, remember?"

"We'll get some hard hats," I promised, "that will make it seem even more of an adventure."

14

The Military had entirely taken over Mo's outer offices, banishing all the usual administrative and secretarial staff. The rooms were crowded with soldiers and equipment and I was virtually invisible to everyone there, unless I asked a question in which case I was immediately treated with suspicion and given no information at all. The doors to the inner office were tightly shut but no one would tell me whether Mo or Lou were inside. I began to wonder if Lou had already persuaded his friend to flee the country.

There were television screens set up, some of which were broadcasting international news channels and others were relaying CCTV camera footage from the streets of the city outside the palace walls, but it was hard to tell which pictures were which. It seemed that the whole world was now watching to see what was going to happen next and there was talk of the people storming the walls in order to flush Mo out. I wondered if Caroline was watching at home. Would she be worried? Should I put her mind at rest? Was that even possible?

I found a corner and sat on the floor to text her. "Hi, don't worry about news coverage, quite safe here. Speak soon. XXX".

As I sent the message off into the ether I had an overwhelming desire to be back home with her. I was beginning to fear that yet again I had showed myself to be reckless and naive. I had blundered unthinkingly into a situation where I was now undoubtedly out of my depth, all for the sake of money. I stood up and scoured the room, trying to spot a face that I might recognise, someone who might help me get to the airport and onto a flight home. Were there even any flights going out at the moment? If there were would they all be full? Maybe I needed to get out and find someone who would drive me over the nearest border. I didn't know who to ask. All the people who had been looking after me ever since I accepted the assignment had disappeared. What about the British Embassy? How could I make contact with them? Were they even still in the country? This sudden torrent of questions was pouring into my brain, tumbling over one another as they picked up speed and found no answers to slow their momentum, propelling me into a cold, sweaty panic.

I'm not sure how long I hung around in those rooms before I realised it was pointless and went back outside. I was yearning for fresh air but there was none. It wasn't just the usual midday heat; there were also the drifting clouds of smoke coming up over the walls. After all the noise inside the offices the gardens seemed shockingly quiet. I stood still and tried to hear the sound of the JCB at work but there was nothing. I moved a little closer to the hedges, trying to avoid gravel paths that might betray my approach, but still I heard nothing. As I hovered for a while on the other side of the hedge I could hear the sound of a sprinkler swishing back and forth. I moved closer to the entrance and eventually I was staring in at the immaculate green lawn which the sprinklers were gently nourishing.

For a second I thought I must have come to the wrong section of the garden. There were so many corners and compartments it was easy to become disorientated – so much "concealment and surprise". Then I wondered if perhaps it had all been a dream or an hallucination. My sleep patterns had been so disrupted for so long now that I perpetually felt I was on the edge of a sort of exhaustion-induced madness. Perhaps I had finally tipped over the edge. I went closer to the grass and bent down to examine it. I could make out the thin lines that showed the turf had been freshly laid, but with the water and the sunshine I knew they would be gone within a few days and there would be absolutely no sign that anything had ever been disturbed. More concealment.

I remembered my first conversation with Lou.

"People have also created a great deal of destruction and ugliness," I had said.

"Not gardeners," he had replied. "Never gardeners. They might make mistakes, of course, but nature will mend them quickly, sometimes within a few months if there is some fertile soil and a temperate climate. Everything is mended by the soil. You can have a battlefield covered in corpses and the next year you have a field of poppies. One day you have an African village piled high with the bodies of the innocent and a few years later you have jungle once more."

But it wasn't nature that had repaired the damage here, it was man with the help of a bulldozer and some carefully cultivated turf. Carnage in the morning replaced by tranquillity by the afternoon. Concealment and surprise.

15

When Caroline saw how excited Becky was at the plan for the tree house she wasn't able to find the heart to protest any more. I could see that it made her horribly nervous whenever Becky and I went out to work with our hard hats balanced ludicrously on the tops of our heads, and she would avoid making eye contact with me every time she was called upon to find a plaster for one or other of us, or to extract a splinter. They were without doubt the happiest times of my life and I felt ridiculously proud of myself for doing something so simple and so constructive and for being able to give Becky so much joy.

During one of our conversations in the palace gardens I asked Lou how he would advise someone to find happiness. He thought for some time before he answered and I can remember his words exactly.

"To achieve happiness I think you have to be able to look back on your past with a sense of pride and look forward to your future with a sense of excitement or anticipation. And you need to be able to do both these things from a position of relative security, perhaps even comfort. Take away any one of those elements and I suspect it is harder to achieve a complete sense of happiness."

His words had made me deeply sad because they had confirmed what I already knew only too well, that I would never be happy again.

"Of course it also depends on your perspective," Lou continued. "A man who has had to sleep in the gutter may be made happy by a simple shelter that you or I would find dispiriting. If you are starting with nothing then there are likely to be more things that can bring you happiness. If you already have a high level of contentment it may be harder because you have a lot to lose."

"Okay," Caroline said when the house was finished and Becky led her proudly out to see the final product. "I admit it, you are both geniuses. But do you think we should just get someone in to check that it is a hundred percent safe?"

"Mum!" Becky exclaimed, expressing affront on both our behalves without me having to say a word. "That is so rude!"

"Okay," Caroline said, raising her hands in mock surrender, "I'm just saying ..."

"Well, don't," Becky said firmly. "Come up and have tea with us instead."

She had laid out a tea party inside the house with dolls' cups and saucers, chocolate biscuits and a teapot full of water. The three of us squeezed in and I could see that Caroline was quite impressed by how solid the structure felt beneath us.

I was in the garden a few days later, trying to find out how the chickens had managed to escape into the vegetables yet again, when the screaming started. Caroline must have been outside too because we were both running towards the tree at the same time and we were both able to see the children falling. Becky had invited her three best friends for the first official tree house tea party after our family event. Since the three of them weighed considerably less than Caroline and I there seemed no reason to assume that it would be any less successful. The structure of the house did indeed hold very firm but a branch of the tree, which I would never for a moment have suspected of harbouring a plan for treachery, did not.

The screaming started at the first sounds of snapping and the first tilting of the structure. The girls didn't actually start falling until a few seconds later and we got there in time for me to catch the third girl and place her safely on the ground while the fourth managed to stay dangling from a lower branch long enough for me to be able to climb the ladder and get her down a few seconds later. It was only as I came back down with the last girl that I took in the fact that Caroline was sitting on the ground stroking Becky's head and another few moments before I was close enough to see that Becky's eyes were closed. The other girl who had hit the ground beside Becky was screaming lustily, making the silence of our daughter's pale lips seem all the more awful in contrast. Many, many times since that terrible moment I have asked myself if it would have been easier or harder to have lived with what happened that day if it had been the other girl, someone else's child, who had been lying silent rather than ours, and it is a question I still have not been able to answer.

I probably only stayed rooted to the ground in horror for a few seconds, but they were long enough seconds for Caroline to have to scream at me to get an ambulance. I instantly followed her orders, running into the house and dialling with trembling fingers. When the voice on the other end asked me for information I panicked that my voice wasn't going to work and that the shaking or the tears were going to overcome it and make me unintelligible at this moment when it was so important to be utterly clear and concise.

16

"I have persuaded Mo that it is time to go." Lou's voice made me jump up guiltily from where I was squatting by the damp grass. "You need to come with us. The guards will not stay loyal forever and once they go the place will be overrun. The helicopter pilots have already vanished."

"Why is Claudia burning all your old pictures?" I asked.

"She is afraid that Mo's enemies will misunderstand the role I played here in the past. Feelings are running high and people are shooting first and asking questions afterwards. It is better not to give them any reason to jump to bad conclusions."

I was unable to stop my eyes from flickering back down to the damp, green grass at our feet.

"Mo wants you to be with him," Lou continued. "He is going to need help telling his story to the world and he thinks you are the best person to do it. He is paranoid and doesn't know who to trust, so say nothing that will make him question your loyalty, at least not until we are all safely away from here. Once he is out of the country he will undoubtedly have more time to devote to talking to you."

"I understand," I said, straightening up and turning away from the sprinklers. "I need to get my things if we are leaving now."

"Do it quickly and come back to the house. We will all go from there together. Don't talk to anyone else. It is impossible to know who is still loyal."

I was surprised to find the extent to which fear was now making it difficult for me to function effectively. Should I run and risk drawing attention to myself, or should I walk fast? I couldn't even make a simple decision like that. I was already out of breath without even exerting any energy. Was I having a panic attack? It was easy to obey Lou's instruction to talk to no one because I wasn't sure I could actually talk coherently as I hurried to my bedroom to grab my laptop and passport. I didn't bother with clothes.

On the way back to Lou's house it seemed to me that the guards were looking at me differently, their eyes narrower and more suspicious, and their fingers closer to their triggers. I told myself I was letting my imagination run away with me and tried to slow down and look as casual as I usually did when strolling around the gardens, but my heart was still thumping as if I was running and my breath was still short. I was too confused to be able to judge if I was looking normal. Lou was herding his family out of the house as I arrived, telling Sanka that she had to leave the bags and lifting the ashen faced girls onto his hips. As we made our way back towards the palace in a group I was sure we were now conspicuous. Sanka was struggling to keep up with all her bags, ignoring Lou's instructions to leave them, and Claudia had pulled a scarf up over her hair which also covered her face. We looked like a bunch of refugees fleeing towards a border, which I guess is exactly what we were becoming. The soldiers were now staring at us openly as we passed them, some of them definitely fingering the triggers of their guns as we made our way into the palace, obviously unsure whether they should challenge us or not. They could make up their minds at any moment.

"Don't catch their eyes," Lou said in a voice that shocked me with its even calmness.

Mo's attitude had changed even more radically than the guards' as he hurried down the staircase to meet us. He looked older and he looked frightened. He was wearing a loose white robe and sandals which slapped on the floor as he walked. I wasn't sure if it was because he hadn't had time to dress properly or whether he was hoping the simple clothes would work as a disguise out on the streets. There were four men with him who I recognised as his most trusted bodyguards. I noticed two soldiers on sentry duty furtively exchanging glances as if asking one another for guidance as to how to react to the man who had been leading their country for more than twenty years but who now looked like a man from the streets.

Before the guards could pluck up the courage to challenge us we had all swept through a door under the staircase with two bodyguards in the lead and the other two bringing up the rear, bolting the door behind us. Stone steps spiralled down into a long, high ceilinged passageway that looked like an indoor stables. There was a well worn cobbled floor and harsh fluorescent lighting illuminated rows of rusty metal doors decorated with heavy metal bolts, most of which were standing open. There was a nauseating stench hanging in the air. As we hurried past I glanced in. They were cells, each one containing much the same things, a bench just long enough for a man to lie on, chains on the walls and sometimes a bucket in the corner. In some of them there were splashes of blood drying on the walls and floor. Even amongst all the panic and hurry, the pieces of the jigsaw were starting to come together in my head. This must have been where the mound of bodies that they were burying in the garden had come from. All the time that I had been strolling with Lou in the beautiful gardens above, there had been unspeakable things going on a few metres beneath our feet, secrets buried too deep in the earth for us to be able to hear the prisoners' screams over the sounds of trickling water. This certainly was the ultimate garden of "concealment and surprise".

We were dashing through the bowels of hell and none of us caught the others' eyes, no one had the breath or words to speak. There was no way I could tell who in our group had known about what went on under the garden or who was working it out for the first time, just as I was.

The bodyguards in the lead seemed to know exactly where we were going as we turned from one corridor to another, each one the same, all of them eerily deserted, until eventually we reached another staircase. The effort of climbing the steps was almost too much for Sanka, who had to stop several times to catch her breath before continuing. Claudia took one of her arms and Lou wordlessly passed the girls to the two bodyguards behind so he could take Sanka's other arm as she clung onto the bags containing her life's possessions. The children looked momentarily alarmed at being passed to virtual strangers but did not protest.

The stairs led us to a door which opened into what looked like a simple house outside the walls of the palace gardens, although there was no furniture and no signs of anyone living in the house. The windows were all shuttered firmly against prying eyes. In a courtyard outside, three anonymous-looking cars were waiting and the grim-faced bodyguards directed us as to which ones to go to. It was a shock to see a world leader like Mo getting into such a vehicle. It was as if he had suddenly been demoted to the ranks of ordinary citizen, and for a second I thought I saw him hesitate as if he was contemplating refusing, as if this was one indignity too far. I had once had the psychology of men in big cars explained to me. If you drive around a poor country in a big, black Range Rover or Mercedes it adds to the image of power and untouchability. It sends a message of awe to those who can probably afford no more than a borrowed bicycle or a lift on a donkey cart. But like the emperor's new clothes, once the illusion of power has been broken such vehicles are exposed for the empty posturing that they really are. They become symbols of extravagance rather than power, delusions of grandeur rather than chariots of the gods. A convoy of black limousines now would seal our fate given the mood of the crowds on the streets. The hunters had become the hunted.

It was obvious we were following a drill that had been immaculately pre-planned. Three of the bodyguards climbed into the driving seats. Lou was sitting in the front seat of one car with Claudia and the children in the back seat. Sanka and I were in the back of the second car, while Mo was in the third with the extra bodyguard. All the bodyguards were in radio contact with one another as we drew out into the street.

It was the first time I had been outside the palace walls since arriving and in those two weeks everything had changed. There were burned-out cars and signs of minor explosions everywhere. Street traders had set up wherever they could amongst the wreckage so that life could continue, but I was suddenly aware of the open drains running with sewage and discarded vegetable leaves and the packs of dogs scavenging in the same territory as the people. The simmering traffic jams which had clogged the roads that had brought me in from the airport just weeks before were gone now and the roads were almost empty of traffic. On my previous trip I had looked out through the darkened windows of the armour plated Mercedes into the bored, resentful eyes of people who were tired of being forced to pull over so that big shiny cars could push through with sirens wailing. One man had been so overcome with fury he had ostentatiously spat at the car, a gob of qat-blackened spittle landing on the window beside my face. The bodyguard's hand had automatically gone to his gun, but two policemen had materialised from the crowd and had bludgeoned the man to the ground, aggressively dispersing the crowd as we sped away.

"Don't worry," the bodyguard had said as he saw the expression on my face, "we are here to look after you." He had then exchanged words with the driver and they had both laughed, like we were playing a game they both enjoyed, one they excelled at.

Now the atmosphere inside the cars was very different. The faces in the crowds that were congregating in the wider avenues that surrounded the palace walls were excited and chanting, hyped up on the hope of finally seeing some changes coming to their sorry lives, frighteningly energised by the noise and danger of the previous few days. They looked like people who expected to overthrow a government and gain from the experience.

The crowds were so dense we often had to slow to a virtual halt and people would peer in at us. I hoped that all they were seeing was ordinary people like themselves trying to get out of the city. After the sumptuously watered grounds of the palace, I was struck by the dryness all around and the withered appearance of the few dust covered trees that had managed to survive the life of the streets. It suddenly seemed inconceivable that there could ever be enough food or water in such a place to succour an entire city's population.

17

In response to my 999 call a paramedic was probably kneeling beside Becky's still body within quarter of an hour of her falling, but that was not how it felt as I stood helplessly by, watching Caroline stroking her head and whispering in her ear. The girl who had been screaming so loudly had calmed down and I tried half heartedly to find out if she had done herself any damage, my eyes seldom leaving Becky's face. The girl was so shocked and confused she kept contradicting herself, but when she tried to stand up one of her legs gave way beneath her and I guessed she had broken it. The other two were in shock but didn't seem to be physically harmed beyond scrapes and scratches. Even though I didn't want to leave Becky and Caroline for a second, being terrified that Becky might open her eyes and ask for me, I ran indoors and grabbed blankets off our bed to wrap them all in while we waited. It wasn't cold but they were all shivering, as were Caroline and I.

One of the girls passed me her phone and said her mother wanted to speak to me. The woman was surprisingly calm and said she would be there as quickly as possible. I asked her to call the mothers of the other two for me. I knew they were all friends and had one another's numbers.

"Tell them the girls are a bit shaken but they aren't hurt," I said. I didn't think I would mention the broken leg until it had been confirmed.

The paramedic was immediately talking over the radio to the ambulance crew. I couldn't understand everything he was saying but I could hear the urgency in his voice as he told them to hurry. A few minutes later we could hear distant sirens and then everything became a blur as the ambulance and a police car and the mothers of the girls all arrived at much the same time, parking haphazardly as everyone rushed about their business. One of the mothers was much more distraught than the others and shouted at the police about how irresponsible Caroline and I were and how we should be prosecuted. Caroline never took her eyes off Becky as the ambulance men carefully scooped her up onto a stretcher and strapped her in tightly, like some precious piece of broken china being packed up and taken away so that delicate repairs could be undertaken. Caroline got into the ambulance with her and I had to stay behind to answer all the questions that the police were obliged to ask so they could do their paperwork. The girl with the broken leg also got into the ambulance and her mother said she would follow in her car. The other two mothers left once the police had taken all their details and the garden suddenly seemed horribly quiet and empty as we went indoors and one of the policemen put the kettle on to make us a cup of tea while they dealt with the paperwork and I tried to stop shaking.

An hour later I was driving to the hospital, following the police car which was going deliberately slowly to make sure I didn't behave rashly in my eagerness to catch up with Caroline and Becky. When we got to the accident and emergency entrance I spotted Caroline sitting on her own in the foyer café, staring into a cup of tea. She didn't respond when I hugged her, her shoulders rigid and her eyes dry.

"She's in the x-ray department," she said before I could even ask. "She hadn't regained consciousness and they are trying to find out what has happened."

I slumped down in a chair beside her and the police hovered in the background until they were called away to another incident on the radio.

"I'm so sorry," I said, hating the weakness of mere words. Caroline stared at me blankly for a second but didn't respond, just going back to staring at her tea. She was in no position to dispense forgiveness.

We didn't speak again for the next two hours, both lost in the horror of our own thoughts. Other people came and went from the café. Visitors, patients, nurses and doctors sat down to eat or drink and then got up to go back to whatever they were doing before. Eventually a young woman in a white coat came and stood beside us. She seemed to know who we were.

"Becky's in the intensive care unit now," she said, "would you like to come and see her?"

We followed the kind, young doctor like zombies. I tried to respond to her comments, wanting to show how grateful we were for whatever she and the others were doing for Becky, but Caroline just stared straight ahead and walked in silence. They had strapped Becky into a bed and there were a number of tubes coming out of her. The young doctor assured us that she was comfortable.

"There's some damage to the spine," she said, "but it will be a while before we know exactly what it is."

"When will she wake up?" I asked, guessing it was a stupid

question but longing for an answer anyway, even if I suspected they were making it up.

"I'm afraid we don't know that either. At the moment we just want to keep her stable and give her body a chance to sort itself out. We'll be able to do more tests soon, then we will know more."

They found us a couple of chairs and we sat either side of the bed, each touching one of the small, bare, pale arms that lay on top of the blanket, both of us staring at her angelic, sleeping face.

18

The car with Mo in it had gone ahead, but we could hear the odd sounds from the second bodyguard's radio over our driver's radio. Every so often I could see the car carrying Lou and his family coming round a corner behind us, then we would turn into another street and I would lose sight of it again. The crowds were moving towards the palace walls from every direction with their banners and their chanting and their fists punching the air. The further we travelled the less people took any notice of a car with an old woman and a nondescript foreign man in the back.

We were on a less populated street, almost out of the city when we heard the gunshots and the shouting over the radio and Sanka began to moan and rock back and forth in her seat. Our driver said nothing but I noticed he had lifted his gun out of its holster and rested it on his lap. I glanced back and saw that a truck full of soldiers had cut in between us and Lou's car, but they seemed not to be taking any notice of either of us. Hopefully we were no more to them than traffic to be navigated around.

Our driver talked to Lou's driver but I didn't catch what they were saying. Two minutes later we saw the roadblock up ahead. Mo's car was standing side on, as if it had been stopped in the middle of trying to do a U-turn and all the doors stood open. I could see the body of one of the bodyguards lying in the dust but the growing crowd of men were ignoring it. They were all pressing in on another body. There were sticks and iron bars rising and falling, like they were restaurateurs beating a kitchen rat to death, ordinary men in shabby clothes shouting furiously, their faces angry but their actions apparently controlled and deliberate.

Our driver slowed down, cradling his pistol in his hand. The truck full of soldiers accelerated past us and came to a stop beside the mob. Some of them turned away from their victim and shook their fists at the soldiers as they dismounted from the truck, but the core of the crowd kept on with the beating as if determined to finish the job before the opportunity had passed.

Lou's car drifted up beside us very slowly and Lou made a discreet hand signal to our driver, apparently telling him to follow them. I could see that Claudia had covered the children's heads with the end of her scarf, which was right across her own face. Sanka was staring at her hands, her fingers fiddling with a set of worry beads in her lap and mouthing a silent prayer over and over, like a mantra. Lou's car nosed its way towards the young soldiers who were now standing around the mob, looking awkward, cradling their guns but apparently unsure what they should do. Their senior officer seemed to be deliberately ignoring the beating and turned his attention to Lou's car, officiously waving it on through, with us trailing in its wake. The officer shouted at some of his men to lift the makeshift roadblock so the traffic could move on. His priority seemed to be to get as many people out of the area as possible.

As we drove past I was unable to stop myself from glancing out of the window at the mob. The ferocity of their blows was lessening, as if their anger was somehow abating. One or two had pulled out mobile phones and were filming the battered and blood soaked corpse lying at their feet. I wouldn't have known it was Mo if it hadn't been for the sandals still on his feet. It looked like there was another body in the background, which I guessed was the second bodyguard.

None of us in the car spoke as the officer waved us through and Lou's car accelerated away ahead of us. There was too much to say and all three of us must have been thinking different thoughts.

We drove for nearly an hour before turning into what looked like a military base. The guards on the gate looked frightened and we waited in silence as we watched Lou talking to them. His hand gestures suggested that he was attempting to calm and reassure them. After what seemed like an age, the barrier went up and Lou nodded quickly to our driver before climbing back into the lead car. We drove through and I saw there was a runway with a small private jet standing in apparent readiness for take-off.

Lou ran up the steps first and was talking to the pilot at the top as the rest of us climbed out of the cars and stood behind him, all of us quiet and shaking. He was explaining that Mo wasn't going to be joining us.

"I have orders to carry His Excellency," the pilot was saying. "I can't leave without him."

"His Excellency is dead," Lou replied, "and it is only a matter of time before the army will realise that things have changed and they will impound this aircraft along with everything else."

The pilot thought for a moment before nodding his understanding of what Lou was saying and going to the cockpit.

The two drivers were already leaving the compound before the door of the aircraft was closed, no doubt heading for the hills, not wanting to fall foul of a mob like their colleagues. If their leader was dead there was no one left for them to protect except themselves.

The flight to Italy did not take long and none of us tried to speak over the roar of the engines; all of us lost in our own thoughts. The hostess whose job it was to look after us obviously had no idea what was going on. To her we were just customers to be fed and watered and smiled at, but she must have wondered why none of us asked for anything and declined her offers of champagne and canapés, hot towels and newspapers. In the end she sat with the children, who she managed to interest in sweets and Cokes.

Lou seemed to have sunk deeper into shock than the rest of us, perhaps because he had been closer to Mo than we had, or perhaps because he had been holding his feelings in the tightest. All his philosophies must have been being stretched to the limit by the sight of his old friend, the man he danced with at Studio 54, being beaten to death by the mob. I wished I could think of something I could say which might make a difference.

19

Lou's family home was just as beautiful and grand as it had looked in the photographs. Having been built for a pope it was well protected by walls that were ancient enough to look like part of the scenery, and it was possible to see for many miles in every direction.

"The Chinese call it 'borrowed scenery,'" Lou had explained to me when I first exclaimed at the view from the terraces. "You see it in all paintings of Chinese gardens; distant mountains or lakes outside the parameters of the garden itself, but part of the bigger picture. Views that a skilled gardener can frame and direct the eye to."

In Lou's absence it seemed that the estate was run by his sister and brother in law, partly as a working vineyard, but also as an exclusive sort of hotel. As a result there were enough bedrooms for us all to be made comfortable the moment we arrived. Shock is surprisingly tiring and I fell asleep the moment I lay down in the room I was taken to, not even bothering to undress.

It was early the following morning that I finally found myself able to text Caroline. I knew it was the right thing to do, even though I was pretty sure she would be too preoccupied with other things to have been following what was happening on the international news. I went outside into Lou's garden and found a seat with a view out over the borrowed scenery of the Tuscan hills. I didn't want her to think that I was expecting any sympathy for the ordeal I had just been through. I had, after all, brought it all upon myself.

"Safely in Italy," I typed, "will be home soon. Love you."

I pressed "send" and sat back to breathe in the fresh morning air and stare across the rows of olive trees on the slopes below the garden, feeling the gentle warmth of the rising sun on the back of my neck. I closed my eyes for a moment and I must have nodded off for a second because the vibration of the phone in my palm made me start. It was a reply from Caroline and my heart actually did miss a beat. I hardly dared to open it for fear of what she might be about to say, but I couldn't bear to delay a second longer to read her words.

"Thank God," she wrote. "I've been so worried. X."

It was hard to believe how one simple X, one minute press of a button by a distant finger, could elicit such a violent reaction in someone. Maybe it was a release of all the pent up emotions of the previous twenty four hours, on top of the horrors of the previous year spent sitting at Becky's side, staring at her unmoving face, willing her to at least blink or sigh or give a cough in protest at the tubes that invaded her body every hour of every day. Reading that single kiss, which might well have been typed out of habit more than love, unleashed a torrent. I wept so uncontrollably that I didn't even hear Lou approaching until he sat down on the old iron seat and put a comforting arm around my shoulders. He didn't ask any questions, he merely sat there and waited until my sobs had subsided and I started to talk. He seemed so calm and strong and paternal, despite all the stress and trauma he had been through in the previous few days. I can completely understand what people mean when they describe someone as being their "rock". Lou was my rock.

I told him pretty much everything from the fall of the tree house to the last time I had seen Becky in her hospital bed. He seemed to understand her medical condition and asked a number of questions which I was able to answer because I had listened to so many doctors explaining to us over the year why there was nothing we could do apart from wait and hope. Every day it became harder to hope, which made both of us all the more determined to continue waiting for as long as it might take. It was hard to talk about it without crying. Even Caroline and I hadn't talked about it much during the year, unless we were asking technical or medical questions of the doctors and nurses. Everything about our daughter's plight was too terrible for us to be able to find adequate words. Caroline had focused nearly all her energies on keeping our daughter's little body clean and healthy in its interminable slumber, while I had concentrated on the practical questions of how we were going to raise the money we were likely to need to look after her for the rest of her life. Telling the whole story again from the start, albeit on a flood of tears, felt strangely cleansing.

"There is a surgeon in California," he said after a while, "who has done some amazing work in the area of the brain and comas."

"Yeah?" I wasn't really listening. We had heard this sort of thing so many times over the previous year. People meant well when they proffered suggestions, they just didn't realise how greedily we would cling to every shred of hope that anyone held out to us, and how devastating it would feel to be disappointed yet again when we tried to follow up whatever the most recent lead was and came to another dead end.

"Would you like me to talk to him? His name is Dan. People generally call him Dr Dan."

I gave a weak smile at the ludicrousness of the name, which I guess he took to be my agreement to the idea and he changed the subject. Ever since the accident had happened Caroline had been dreaming of being able to fly Becky back to America. Her love affair with the old fashioned romantic ideal of England, which she had found in Arnold Petteridge's house when she first arrived in London, had not survived her experiences in the National Health hospital where we now spent most of our family life. She had no complaints about any of the staff or anything that was being done to Becky medically, but a suffocating air of shabbiness filled the worn down Victorian building and stifled all optimism. From the paint on the walls to the smells from the kitchens, from the harsh lights to the empty echoing corridors, everything seemed designed to lower the spirits of all who entered, and to remind them that everyone's days are numbered, without providing any inspiration to enjoy whatever life might be left to them. It was a place of many small kindnesses but not a place of hope. Her memories of early experiences of the American healthcare system were very different, but she had been forced to accept that such treatment was only available to people who had endless access to money or health insurance. We had neither, so we had both accepted that taking Becky to America for some miracle cure had to remain a dream until I had managed to raise a small fortune.

"We've booked you a flight back to England this evening," Lou went on. "Is that okay? We will run you over to Pisa Airport this afternoon."

"Thank you."

I longed to see Caroline and Becky more than anything in the world. In fact the thought of even having to wait another day was hard to bear. Was it just because of that single X in the text? Had that reignited all my hopes? Was I bound to end up disappointed and rejected again, sent straight back to the dog house that I knew I so richly deserved to be in and from which only she could release me?

"Before you go Zana has asked to meet you."

"She's here?"

"She's on her way from Milan with the girls. They will be safer here for the next few weeks."

I had not met Zana, but I felt like I had. Mo had often talked about her, and I had done some research into her background. I knew that before she met and married Mo she had been a successful investment banker. I knew that her father was an Indian diplomat and her mother was French. They had met when he was posted to Paris. I had seen pictures of her and the two daughters that she and Mo had together, and knew that they were beautiful.

"We got out just in time," Lou was saying. "They stormed the palace an hour after we left. All the news bulletins have been covering the destruction."

"What about your garden?"

"Mostly they have concentrated on the house. Even angry mobs tend to be respectful of gardens. Whether they will receive the care and attention they need after the change of regime is another matter of course. Hopefully some of the staff will stay on until things are stable once more and they will be able to resume the work."

"I'm sorry," I said.

"Sorry for what?"

"Sorry that you have lost your friend and your perfect life."

"Thank you," he said, apparently genuinely touched that I should realise how much he had lost, "but there is plenty to be done here. My sister has been nagging me for years to come back and take care of my own garden. Now I can do that. I am lucky to have a family to come back to. Perhaps I shall end my days here, where I started. It seems like the right thing. Roots are important, don't you think? I am old to be the father of young girls, but at least when I go they will be part of a larger family. Perhaps the time was right for Mo and me to part. Claudia and the girls are my only responsibility now."

20

Two large black Mercedes slid up to the house a couple of hours later. I was still sitting in the garden so I was able to watch as bodyguards jumped from the front seats and opened the rear doors to allow Zana from the first car and her two daughters from the second. Staff bustled out of the house as the trunks of the cars opened automatically to allow access to a great many matching suitcases.

All three women were wearing dark glasses and none of them showed any sign of being unduly ruffled by the recent turn of events in their home country. They all looked as if they had just come from the hairdressers and were now on their way to lunch in a smart restaurant somewhere. Perhaps if you have to live with the constant awareness that your husband or father might be assassinated, you are able to prepare a façade that will hold up when the moment finally comes. The dark, cool interior of the house swallowed them up out of the sunshine and once emptied of the luggage the two Mercedes crept away round the house and out of sight, their mission accomplished.

I think the girls may have been more upset by events than their mother, because they had not come down from their rooms for lunch by the time Lou escorted me into the dining hall, a room that was actually more like a medieval church, with its ancient stonework, vaulted ceilings and a great many candles. It was easy to imagine that popes and emperors had once sat in such a room.

Zana was as immaculate, charming and unruffled as it was possible for any woman to be. When Lou introduced us she held onto my hand with her small, cool fingers as if to ensure I didn't escape before she'd had a chance to say what was on her mind. I was aware of her perfume as she held me at arm's length.

"Both Lou and Mo have spoken so highly of you," she said, "and I want to thank you for all you are doing to correct the lies that are being told about Mo. He needs friends like you and Lou more than ever now that he can no longer speak in his own defence. We need to ensure that his legacy is not tainted by a misinformed media. So many people who did not know him seem to want to air their ignorance."

She had succeeded in simultaneously enchanting, flattering and slightly horrifying me. I was enchanted by her grace and beauty, flattered by her words and horrified that I had in some way been awarded responsibility for protecting Mo's legacy.

Eventually she let go of my hand and we sat down for lunch with Lou and Claudia.

"The book must still be published," Zana said, placing the tiniest amount of mozzarella on the tip of her tongue before putting down her fork as if her part in the meal was now completed. Lou and Claudia continued to eat heartily and I followed their example, suddenly hungry as the adrenalin upon which I had been living for so long was finally subsiding.

"I still don't really have enough of Mo's own words for a full book," I confessed. "He had a lot on his mind during the time I was with him."

"Could it perhaps be a biography rather than an autobiography?" Lou suggested. "There must be plenty of material out there. Zana and I could both fill in any gaps for you."

"I'm not sure that I am really qualified to write a biography that anyone would take seriously," I said. "I am known as a ghost, not an historian or even a journalist. I have difficulty with deciding what I actually believe about anything, so I would be happier writing it in his words. I find writing objectively almost impossible, but by using his voice I can be wholly subjective and convincing, hopefully."

"What if you ghosted it for me?" Zana asked, taking the daintiest of sips from her water glass. "What if we wrote it as my memoir of my husband? I think that could be very charming. I could talk about the private side of him, the side that no one outside the family saw. He really could be a very sweet man, you know."

"He was very much in love with you," I said, and then blushed. "I'm sorry, that sounds like flattery, but it's true."

"I know," she smiled so sweetly that I was completely able to understand why Mo had felt the way he did about her. "That's what I mean. He was a good husband and a good father too."

"He was a dutiful son as well," Lou added.

"That's true," she agreed, "he was dutiful, despite being tested in the extreme. People forget that. They forget what a tyrant his father was. Mo did a wonderful job of expunging those painful memories for the next generation. So will you do that, will you write a book for me instead of Mo? We have a house in London and I will be settling there as soon as it is safe to travel. We could meet there to talk."

"Certainly," I said, although at that moment all I could think about was getting on a plane back to Caroline and Becky, and it seemed to me like Zana was simply making polite conversation. I did not expect to ever hear from her again.

21

The house and garden had an abandoned feel to them when I arrived home. I hadn't told Caroline exactly when I would be arriving, not wanting her to feel that she had to make any special arrangements about picking me up or stocking the house with food. From the musty smell that greeted me as I pushed open the front door it didn't feel as if anyone had been there much while I had been away. I imagined she must have been at the hospital most of the time. Even though we had communicated very little since the accident, having someone else in the house did at least make it seem a little alive. The emptiness and silence of the rooms once I had closed the door behind me was frightening. It must have been intolerable when it was just her, on her own. Even the sad, bleak bustle of the hospital ward would have been preferable, and she would have wanted to be close to Becky every moment that she could. I doubted if she had cooked herself a single meal since I'd gone, existing on sandwiches from the hospital café.

I wondered if she would resent me for coming back and disrupting her routine with Becky. Even entering the house felt slightly as if I was an outsider, invading her private world. I stood at the window and stared out at the damp, overgrown garden. All the animals had been found new homes so there was no movement in any of the collapsing pens. The lawn had not been touched since I left and, fuelled by a steady drizzle, it was on its way to returning to meadowland, the lush grass weighed down by the weight of the water. There was a gentle aroma of rotting vegetation in the air and it all seemed a million miles from the dry, manicured perfection of the palace grounds or the warm golden views from Lou's Tuscan terrace.

The urge to see them was overwhelming and the thought of waiting in the silence of the house for Caroline to return, having no idea how long that would take, was suddenly unbearable. I called a taxi which had arrived by the time I had showered and changed.

The hospital had fallen into its night time routines; pools of light on nurses' desks in the darkness, small coloured lights blinking on the machines which churned constantly on, the occasional sound of heels on corridor floors echoing unnaturally and disturbingly in the gloomy hush. Caroline was sitting beside the bed reading a book with a small overhead light that lit one side of her beautiful face, making her look thinner than I remembered, her eyes bigger and her fine cheekbones even higher. There was a familiar fluttering of butterflies in my stomach at the sight of her.

I bent down to kiss her and she raised her hand, the tips of her fingers making contact for a second with my cheek, sending a surge of hope through my whole body.

"Hi," she whispered, out of respect for the other sleeping patients.

I leant over the bed to kiss Becky. She looked exactly the same.

"How is she?" I asked.

"No change."

I sat down and put my hand over Becky's for a few moments.

"I saw your friend being killed on the television," Caroline said.

"He was never my friend, just a client. But I had grown to quite like him in a way, even though he had done many terrible things."

"No one deserves to die like that."

"A lot of other people had died just as painfully on his watch."

As we both returned to watching Becky as she slept Caroline held my other hand and I felt a tiny flicker of warmth and gratitude somewhere deep inside.

22

It took me a few moments to recall who "Dr Dan" was when I saw the email in my in-box. Lou's comment about the surgeon he knew in California had been so fleeting that I had not thought about it again.

"Our mutual friend, Lou, has told me about your daughter, Becky," the email read. "Of course I cannot make any promises but we have been making big strides forward with these sorts of cases in recent months and I would be very happy to see Becky at my hospital here in Los Angeles if you and your wife feel it would be appropriate."

I emailed back to tell him how grateful I was for the offer, and felt a familiar wave of self-disgust as I went on to confess that there was no way I could find the money to fly a comatose Becky all the way to the west coast of America. His response was almost immediate.

"It is my understanding," he said, "that Lou would be happy to undertake the costs of bringing Becky here with you and your wife, as well as the costs of any operation and hospital care. If my understanding is correct and that makes any difference to your decision, my offer still holds."

I had to re-read the email several times before I could be completely sure that I had understood it. The costs of flying Becky and all her life support systems, presumably with nurses or doctors in attendance all the way, and then the costs of Dr Dan and his state-of-the-art hospital, were likely to stratospheric. Was Lou really offering to pay for all that? Could he even afford it? I knew he was a wealthy man but this would be an enormous gesture of kindness to someone he hardly even knew.

Caroline was washing a load of Becky's laundry from the hospital when I came through with print-outs of the emails. She preferred to do it herself, so that it would smell like home for her.

"You remember I told you about the Italian guy who got me out of the palace?" Over the previous few weeks I had started to tell her a little about what I had seen and what I had heard but she had not shown anything more than a polite interest in any of it.

"The gardener who was a friend of the President?"

"Yeah, Lou. Well, he knows a surgeon in California who specialises in a new technique for bringing people out of comas and he has offered to fly Becky over there. At least I think he has."

The washing was forgotten as she snatched the emails from my hand and bombarded me with questions.

"Let's Google them both," she said eventually, unsatisfied with the depth of my knowledge on both Lou and Dr Dan.

She did the Googling while I sat beside her, watching and waiting, trying to read and digest the things she brought up on the screen before she flicked impatiently on to the next and the next, too fast for me to keep up.

"Your friend Lou is a bit of a dark horse," she said eventually.

"I know," I said, not sure what part of Lou's history she was referring to.

"It seems that he was in charge of all the arms purchases for your friend, the President."

"I told you, he wasn't my friend."

She ignored my protest, too fired up with her own train of thought as her fingers flew over the keyboard.

"I think Lou was the middleman for virtually every tank, every gun and every uniform that the army purchased for about twenty years. He must have been on commission for all these deals. He basically provided the weaponry needed to keep your friend in power."

I didn't bother to protest again, suspecting that she was using the term on purpose to remind me of just how far I had sold out on my principles.

"Not only that," she went on, "he also seems to have been instrumental in some really dodgy oil deals in the former Soviet Union. His name comes up in articles about pipelines being laid through countries which caused the displacement of enormous numbers of people. There are stories of whole villages being massacred if they refused to move into refugee camps when told to. There are several human rights organisations that have had him on a blacklist for years."

I felt a cold chill passing through me. Was this how Claudia and Sanka came into the picture?

"If you met him ..." I said, my voice trailing feebly off as she turned with an arched eyebrow.

"There were plenty of people who thought Hitler was absolutely charming."

"Oh, come on," I protested. "Hitler?"

The eyebrow stayed up in a curve so perfect Leonardo Da Vinci couldn't have improved on it. So many times I had come close to telling her about the piles of bodies I had seen in Lou's "garden of concealment and surprise", and how they had been made to disappear in hours beneath the lawns. I had lain awake at night after nightmares, longing to share the burden. The secret hovered like an invisible wall between us and I knew that I would feel better if I smashed it down. I also knew that if I now spoke openly about such things the option of accepting Lou's offer of help for Becky might close forever. She was continuing to type and bring up new documents, her fingers moving too fast for me to be able to follow what was happening on the screen, her concentration so intense she couldn't see whatever agonies of indecision might be registering in my face as I sat beside her and waited miserably for the next revelation. I became aware that she had stopped at a particularly densely printed page and was studying the words so intensely that her lips were actually moving silently as she read. I leant forward to try to see what she had found but couldn't make sense of the mass of grey print.

"He's mentioned on this blog as being involved in the arming of the Chinese Army," she said eventually, her tone more than a little triumphant.

"The Chinese Army? Aren't they the world's biggest employers of manpower or something?"

"About three million on the payroll," she said, still reading as she talked. "Which would mean a pretty good percentage cut for anyone involved in supplying them. Any idea what 'microwave weapons' might be?" I shook my head. "Or 'particle beam weapons'? Or 'electromagnetic pulse weapons'?"

"No. You might as well be talking Chinese." It was a feeble attempt at a joke, which she appeared not to have heard.

"He also seems to have been involved in the Chinese Army's commercial enterprises which were devolved during the

Nineties. That would put him on a par with the Russian oligarchs who bought up the Soviet State enterprises for peanuts – only maybe his deals were on a bigger scale."

"Okay," I tried to stay calm. I couldn't afford to back either of us into some sort of debating corner which would mean we missed an opportunity for Becky just to prove a moral point. "Let's accept all this stuff at face value for a moment. Are we saying that we are going to refuse his offer of help? Are we going to turn down this possibility, however, thin, that this Dr Dan actually does know something the others don't?"

She paused for a second, fingers hovering above the keys.

"Let's Google Dr Dan, then."

23

Even Caroline had to admit that what Lou had laid on for us was impressive. A private ambulance picked us and Becky up from the hospital and two nurses and two paramedics accompanied us all the way to an airport a couple of hours' drive away, where an ambulance plane was waiting on the tarmac. All of us were travelling together to Los Angeles. I actually caught myself wishing that Becky was awake so that she too could enjoy the drama and sheer extravagance of the whole adventure, all being done for her. It already felt like we were progressing, just to see her outside the sterile and ugly surroundings of the hospital ward, away from the overpowering smells of sickness and antiseptic. The plane smelled more like an expensive hotel bedroom.

"You realise that by doing this he is hoping to buy your loyalty and your discretion," Caroline had said at some point during the long hours that we had spent wrestling with our consciences, during which I had finally confessed to everything I had seen at the palace. "He knows you saw those bodies being buried in the garden."

I think both of us knew that we were going to accept Lou's offer from the first moment he made it, certainly from the moment when we saw Dr Dan's website and read the articles he had published, but that didn't stop us from constantly revisiting the decision, pressing at it like you might press a fading toothache to check if it still hurts. She had known I was holding back something and I tripped up under her intense questioning, unable to keep hold of any secrets now that we were sharing things again. I kept telling her that I had no proof about any of it, that I might even have dreamed it. She wasn't fooled for a second, any more than I was.

"I do realise that," I said, "And I don't think there is anything I can do to change it."

"You would be a valuable witness for anyone trying to pin a charge of Crimes Against Humanity on him."

"Yes, I suppose I would."

"But not if you have accepted a gift this generous."

"I understand all that. But imagine if Dr Dan can get Becky to wake up. Imagine that, Caro, and see if you can bring yourself to turn the opportunity down."

In the end there had been no contest for either of us but that didn't mean that we weren't feeling bad about it even as we sank into the comfort of the reclining seats and allowed the infinitely kind and capable medical staff to take over at Becky's bedside.

Another ambulance was waiting for us on the tarmac in Los Angeles and we were hurried through the passport and immigration procedures by our small army of minders.

"Is this what life is like for your friends all the time?" Caroline asked and I saw a sparkle of mischief in her eyes which I had feared I would never see again.

"Pretty much," I grinned, "and will you please stop calling them my friends."

She gave me a sceptical look as the sirens ignited on the roof of the ambulance and we sped out of the airport and through the California traffic to Dr Dan's hospital in the hills.

It felt more like arriving at a spa resort as the ambulance killed its siren and slid under the covered portico. We were met by a team of nurses with the beaming smiles and the figures of film actresses and we were ushered gently into Dr Dan's consulting room while they wheeled Becky away to make her comfortable. Dr Dan was waiting for us with another welcoming smile and a handshake so strong and firm you just knew he was capable of achieving anything he put his mind to. Caroline practically melted before my eyes as he ushered us into armchairs and plied us with coffee, orange juice and croissants.

We talked like old friends and his understanding of what we had been through made both of us well up and make use of the strategically placed boxes of ridiculously soft tissues. He managed to extract a medical history from us in an hour which was more rounded and detailed than anything any of the doctors or nurses we had been living amongst for the last year would have known about. We signed the disclaimer forms that he asked for and then the three of us went together to see Becky, who lay serenely in a pure white room with views out across the city and down to the distant, blue ocean. The sun was shining and the room was scented by a gigantic bunch of white flowers bearing a good luck card from Lou and Claudia.

Caroline was leaning against me like she used to when we walked home from evenings out in the early years of our relationship. I put my arm around her shoulders and she looked up at me with grateful, teary eyes. Dr Dan examined Becky, talking to her quietly and encouragingly as if he were quite sure she could hear. Eventually he seemed satisfied and stepped back from the bed.

"What a lovely girl," he said, "you must both be very proud."

We both nodded, unable to find words to express how we felt and how grateful we were to him for lifting the weight of our worries so apparently effortlessly. At that moment nothing else in the world seemed remotely important.

"I would like to schedule Becky in for a procedure this afternoon," he said, guiding us out of the room. "So we have organised a room for you down the hall where you can rest if you want to, or you could take advantage of the gardens or the canteen. If you want to go out anywhere for a few hours just tell them at reception and they will arrange for one of the drivers to look after you."

The room he showed us was very like the one Becky was in, but without all the medical equipment. There was another bunch of flowers from Lou and Claudia. Dr Dan withdrew and left us alone. We flopped down on the bed and Caroline laid her head on my chest. After a few moments she started laughing.

"What are you laughing at?"

"I'm sorry. I just can't believe this place. It's like we've walked onto the set of some Californian soap opera."

Her laughter set me off and a few minutes later we were making love for the first time since the accident. It felt sweet and gentle, full of reminders of happy times. It was partly a celebration of the renewal of our mutual hope and partly an escape from the reality of our shared unhappiness. It left both of us exhausted and shuddering with relief.

24

We fell asleep after making love and when we woke and ventured out to see Becky we found that her room was empty, the bed and all its attendant machinery miraculously vanished. Both of us gave sharp intakes of breath, suddenly frightened and suddenly guilty for not being there at the moment she disappeared, for indulging ourselves when we should have been guarding her.

"Dr Dan is with Becky in surgery right now," a nurse informed us.

"Everything is going well."

She suggested we might like to have something in the canteen while we waited but neither of us thought we could face eating, our stomachs now tight with anxiety. On the one hand it was wonderful to have all the responsibility lifted from our shoulders for a while, there really was nothing we could do to influence what might happen over the next few hours, but at the same time it was unnerving to be so disempowered.

We wandered out into the garden which had been designed along Japanese lines to bring peace and harmony to troubled patients, all water over pebbles and beautifully raked patterns in the coloured gravel. There were seats in the shade with the same views we had seen from the windows. It would have been a lovely place to sit if you were recuperating from an operation, but the beauty and tranquillity were lost on us as we spent most of our time staring at the door to the hospital, waiting from someone to bring us news.

Every so often a nurse would come out to find out if there was anything we needed and to give us positive bulletins on what was going on in the operating theatre. After what seemed like a lifetime of waiting they told us that Dr Dan would be with us soon. He emerged a few minutes later looking as fresh and groomed as he had looked when we arrived. There was no way of telling that he had just spent several hours bent over an operating table doing the most intricate of brain surgery. He smiled at us reassuringly as he pulled up a seat opposite us and took Caroline's hands in his, staring into her eyes as he spoke.

"I am so sorry," he said, his smile replaced with an expression of the deepest regret imaginable. "I'm afraid we lost her. Becky passed away just half an hour ago."

25

From that moment there seemed to be no point for either of us in anything. Everything was desolation, the spectacular view and the warm sunshine vanished in a second. We sat shivering together in the Japanese garden after Dr Dan had gone back inside, not having the slightest idea what we should do or say to one another next. I put my arm round Caroline's shoulder and she leant her full weight against me as if even sitting upright was now too painful. Becky had been our future, and as long as she was still breathing she had been the reason for us to continue struggling through the long days and nights. Now that reason had gone.

A gentle, solicitous staff came looking for us like we were now the patients, helping us to do the things we had to do. They took us to see her and she looked no different to the last time we had seen her, except that now she wore a little hood to hide her shaved head, and all the tubes had gone, leaving her free to float away from us. We both held her hands for a while, trying to tether her to us for just a little longer. Neither of us ever wanted to let her go, but both of us knew we were going to have to. We were too shocked to even cry.

Dr Dan must have contacted Lou because when we were finally persuaded to tear ourselves away from the bedside we were told that a room had been booked for us at a nearby hotel. If we would like to make our wishes known they would make all the necessary arrangements. If we would like them to make suggestions that too could be facilitated. Neither of us could make any decisions so we asked to be taken to the hotel so we could gather our thoughts and decide what to do next.

We rang Caroline's parents and they suggested that we fly Becky home to them on the East Coast, and bury her there in a family plot. Caroline seemed to like that idea and anything that she liked I was more than willing to go along with. For all the differences I might have had with my own parents when they were alive, I would have liked to have had them there to lean on at that moment and I was grateful to Caroline's family for treating me the same as her. I think I expected them to blame me for the whole thing, just as I blamed myself, but if they did think it was my fault they showed no sign of it to me. We all seemed to be soaked in the same overwhelming sadness at the loss and I don't know how I would have coped with the agony of the funeral and the little coffin that separated me from Becky if I had not been surrounded by such kind and understanding people.

Neither Caroline or I felt any inclination to return to the house in England. What would be the point? What would be the point of even pruning a tree or planting a bulb if Becky was never going to be there to see the results? Eventually Caroline's father took me to one side and pointed out that if we didn't intend to live in the house then we should let it or sell it, or make some other arrangement.

"You and Caroline still have to live," he said, "even if you don't believe you want to at the moment. Go back to England and sort out your affairs. It will help to give you at least some closure on this chapter of your lives. Leave Caroline here with her mother for a while. We'll look after her till you get back."

I could see the sense in what he was saying, and I had nothing else with which to fill my days and distract myself from my own misery, so that was how I came to be in England when my mobile phone rang and Zana invited me to lunch in London the following day.

"I have some personal problems at the moment..." I said, not feeling like going back to that adventure, any more than I felt like doing anything else.

"I heard," she said, "I am so sorry for your loss. But I need your help. Just come for lunch, what harm can it do?"

"I'm not sure that I would be able to write at the moment."

"I understand," she said, obviously determined not to give up. "Just come for lunch, that's all I'm asking, as a friend."

Since we had only ever met once I didn't for a moment feel that I was her friend, but at the same time I was ridiculously flattered that she would feel she could use such a word. Coming back to the empty house on my own had brought my spirits down to an all time low and the thought of the distraction of some company over lunch was surprisingly attractive.

The first few times that the estate agents brought viewers to the house I had stayed around, doing all the things they tell you in the magazine articles like brewing coffee to fill the rooms with a tempting aroma and putting fresh flowers in the vases. None of it fooled anyone and it was painful to hear the house where I had once experienced more happiness than anywhere else, being discussed by strangers who had no reason to be polite and who saw nothing other than decay and bodged building work. The fences in the garden that Becky and I had spent so many hours mending now sagged under the weight of entangled weeds, and patches on the walls which we had covered with cheap plastic frames filled with families photographs were now exposed for what they were, evidence of a leaky roof. After the first couple of viewings I made a point of going out for long walks whenever the estate agents announced they were coming, following the same routes that we used to go on as a family on sunny afternoons, unable to think of anything less painful to do.

Having not wanted to talk to anyone since that terrible day in California, I suddenly felt in need of some time outside my own thoughts. I wondered if this was a tiny sign that something inside my head might finally be showing signs of healing over – and that thought instantly made me feel guilty. When I woke the next morning I was shocked to find that I felt excited at the thought of taking some trouble over my shaving, putting on some smarter clothes and going off to the bustling big city for another small adventure, particularly as I no longer felt any obligation to agree to anything Zana might propose. Now that Becky was gone there was no longer any need to earn money. I did not need to worry about building a pot of capital to look after her for the rest of her life should she need looking after. The last reason for continuing to live had now gone, along with the last reason to care.

26

Zana's house was in Belgravia, the sort of mighty, white wedding cake of a Georgian house that you see written about in the papers as being worth tens of millions of pounds. I made a polite, and sincere, comment about the beauty of the house and the square that it stood in and she seemed genuinely pleased.

"Yes," she said. "It is lovely round here. There are so many nice shops and restaurants. It's like living in a village."

The idea of a village where all the inhabitants belonged to the international super-rich made me laugh. She looked surprised by my reaction, but I was even more surprised. It was a sound I had not heard coming from my throat for a long time. We sat for a while in a yellow sitting room, with a line of windows twelve feet high allowing sunshine to pour in from above the trees outside, making small talk. I told her about my tribulations with estate agents and people coming to view the house, and she told me how difficult it was for her girls to meet marriageable men when they were always travelling from place to place. As we talked I found my old professional curiosity unfurling back into life like a new spring leaf after a long cold winter.

"How did you and Mo meet?"

"He didn't tell you?" She seemed slightly offended but not altogether surprised.

"He told me bits," I back-tracked, "but he wasn't very good at talking about the personal stuff."

"I can quite imagine. It was a skiing party. We were all staying at the Palace Hotel in Gstaad. Do you know it?"

"No."

"Mo and Lou were with a bunch of other people, mostly Italians I think. There were some very beautiful women in the group I remember. I was on holiday with my family. I had finished university and I was just starting work at one of the French investment banks and my father wanted us all to spend New Year together. Mo was about ten years older than me and he seemed very glamorous."

"Did you know who he was?"

"Good Lord no. I'm not sure I would even have known who his father was at that stage. I had led a very sheltered life; my father had made sure of that. I think he was hoping to arrange a marriage for me with a family in India, but my mother put a stop to any talk of that, thank goodness. She was French you know."

"Yes, I know."

"The French are a romantic race, they do not believe in practical things like arranged marriages. It would be anathema to them."

It was her turn to laugh then. It sounded as if she was fond of her parents. I imagined they were probably still a close family. Off in the distance I heard the sounds of the front doorbell, people were being let in but Zana kept talking without a flicker of interruption until the manservant who had brought me up arrived again to announce two more guests. One was the Minister I had met when my name was first put forward for the job; the other was the senior lawyer who had overseen the meeting in London where I had signed all the confidentiality papers. I felt a little put out that my conversation with Zana had been interrupted in this way, but at the same time intrigued. There were a hundred more questions I wanted to ask her about meeting and marrying Mo, but the arrival of these two raised a great many new questions. Unsure quite where to start, I stayed silent and waited to see what would happen next.

"There is so much that you should be writing about my country now," the Minister said as he held onto my hand for a surprisingly long time, staring into my eyes as if wanting to hypnotise me. "I am going to be writing again now. It is important to explain to the world what is truly happening. People need to understand what is truly going on."

The lawyer deliberately distracted his attention as if wanting to stop him saying any more and I became invisible for a while as they talked amongst themselves. It seemed that the Minister had somehow managed to hold onto his job, despite being an integral part of Mo's team, or at least he certainly didn't seem unduly perturbed by events, and he and the lawyer gave the impression of being comfortable in one another's company, as if their relationship went back a long way and involved a lot of private jokes which they had no intention of sharing with me.

The white-coated manservant, who came and went from the room with barely a sound overseeing the two young waiters who brought us platters of raw vegetables and whatever drinks we asked for, informed Zana that lunch was ready whenever she was. She nodded her understanding and all the servants disappeared, closing the double doors silently behind them. The two men hardly registered I was there as they politely jousted with one another for Zana's attention. She allowed them to continue for a moment before reminding them that I was there.

"I think we should tell our friend here about our plans," she said.

"Can I just say one thing," the lawyer interrupted, looking directly at me, "anything that might be discussed here today would be covered by the non-disclosure agreement that you signed with us at the beginning."

"I understand," I said, although I wasn't sure I did yet.

"Mo has left a considerable fund of money," Zana said, "more than the girls and I could ever possibly need. We are very anxious that it should be used in Mo's name for the good of the country. It was Lou's idea actually."

"What was Lou's idea?" I experienced an unsettling lurch of emotion at the reminder of Lou's existence. The last time I had seen his name it had been on a card in a bunch of flowers in Dr Dan's clinic.

"To turn the country into one giant garden," Zana said.

"To make the desert bloom," the Minister threw his arms wide and laughed joyously at the thought of just how wonderful this plan was.

"It would start with irrigation projects," the lawyer explained quietly. "Building desalination plants, piping water to the villages, diverting rivers, maybe creating canals, whatever it takes to ensure that the water gets to the right places."

"Then we will encourage smallholders of all sorts," Zana picked up his thread. "The idea is to make the people self sufficient. Once they are well fed and well watered, and in control of their own destinies and those of their families, then the whole country will be in a position to move forward, raising material living standards, improving roads."

"Mo left enough money for this to happen?"

"There is substantial seed money," the lawyer said, cautiously and, I thought, a little smugly, as if wanting me to understand that he was used to dealing in such mind boggling amounts.

"It is what he would have wanted for the country he loved," Zana said, "for the people he loved."

I could hear Caroline's voice in my head, asking why, if that was what Mo had wanted, he hadn't directed the money into such projects when he was in power, rather than directing it to Swiss banks. But, given that he hadn't done that and the situation was as it was; wasn't this a good opportunity to make a difference, to do something really worthwhile?

"Let's go through and eat," Zana said and the three of us followed her lead towards the doors which swung silently open upon our approach.

27

"Zana told me it was your idea to involve me in this scheme," I said as I walked with Lou along the rows of vines, stopping every so often for him to tie up a loose end or snip off a piece of dead wood.

"Yes. You seem like a man who needs a project. You would be good at it too."

"Is this whole thing your idea?"

"It's certainly something I have been thinking about for a while. And talking about with colleagues who are in a position to help."

"Did you talk to Mo about it?"

"Often. He liked the idea."

"But not enough to do anything about it."

"The problem for Mo, and most people in positions of genuine power, is that there is no time in their lives for prolonged thought. He liked the ideas of making the country bloom again, but something else more urgent always came along to distract him. Politics eats away the time of leaders. The world needs to find a way to give them more space to think and dream."

"He had time to channel a lot of money into Switzerland."

"Such transactions do not take up much time," Lou said without even glancing up from the branch he was tying up. "If he had taken more time over that he might have seen that he was going in the wrong direction."

"How much money did he squirrel away while he was in power?"

This time he straightened up and turned to me. After a moment he smiled. "Asking the right questions is one of the greatest life skills a man can develop."

"Roughly how much?" I persisted, ignoring the flattery which I guessed was meant to distract me.

"Very hard to pin the amounts down because they change all the time with currency fluctuations, interest rates ...."

"Lou," I interrupted, becoming impatient with him for the first time ever, "if you are planning to transform an entire country you must have at least a rough idea of the budget at your disposal."

"There is enough for the job."

"Billions?"

"Oh, certainly."

"But isn't this like a mugger offering to pay his victim a pension out of his ill gotten gains? Should the money not simply be handed back to the people it was stolen from for them to decide what to do with it?"

The mugger analogy had actually come from Caroline when I was trying, very ineffectively, to explain to her via Skype what had transpired at the house in Belgravia and why I had left the lunch feeling inexplicably elated.

"And are you confident the people you hand it back to would do the right thing?" Lou asked.

"Who's to say what the right thing is?"

"Quite, and while everyone argues over what the right thing might be, the money vanishes with no gain to anyone."

He fell silent, snipping irritably at the vines. It was the first time I had seen him even close to losing his temper. I suppressed the urge to say any more, waiting to see what he would say next.

"There is other money available apart from the funds Zana has access to," he said at last. "But it would be better not to confuse the picture with too many details of international finance. People like simple stories with intriguing beginnings, gripping middles and inspiring ends. That's right, isn't it?"

He glanced at me and still I fought the urge to say anything. I didn't even nod to show that I accepted what he was saying.

"There is a great deal of money in the world at the moment," he continued, regaining his composure and talking more like the old teacher I had first met in the palace garden. "It is not always clear exactly who it belongs to. Sovereign wealth funds need to find places to invest in order to spread their risks. None of this is likely to be of interest to the general reading public. They are going to like the idea of a murdered leader posthumously ploughing his money back into the soil of his own country in order to create a prosperous future for the people who assassinated him, showing compassion and forgiveness. That is a great story, is it not? That is how Mo would like to be remembered."

"It could be a great story," I said, already able to see the structure of it forming in my head, "but is it the truth?"

We continued to walk in silence until he turned up towards the house.

"Come. There's someone I would like you to meet. You'll learn a lot."

The elderly Chinese woman who was sitting with the women and children in the kitchen only came a little above my waist when she stood up and she had a handshake that was as light as the flutterings of a baby bird.

"This is Li," Mo said, "the greatest gardener in the world."

"Your lunch guest is already in the dining room," Claudia said. "He wanted to send some emails so I took him in there."

"Let's go through and find him," Lou said, conducting us all through to the dining hall where a middle aged Indian man in a business suit was bent over his computer, typing. He jumped up like an old fashioned school boy as we came in and Lou greeted him with what seemed to be genuine warmth.

"This is my good friend, Khan," he said as he drew the man towards me and Li. "He runs the biggest aggro chemicals business in the world. He is the one who is truly making the world bloom."

Li gave a deep and respectful bow as Claudia guided us all towards our designated seats in what seemed to be a more carefully choreographed plan than it might have appeared on the surface and I found myself sitting next to the ever smiling Li.

"So," I said to my neighbour, when the food had been distributed and the level of conversation had risen round the table, "what is the greatest secret of gardening do you think?"

"Oh," her smile broadened even further and she rested her fingers lightly on mine for emphasis. "Water is the most important. Without fresh water nothing else will happen."

"Li has very kindly offered to build some desalination plants for us," Lou interrupted from across the table. "Extracting fresh water from sea water is going to be as important this century as extracting oil from the rocks below was in the last century. Once we have the water then Khan can work magic with his chemicals and Li can design paradise on Earth for everyone."

Li's raised her fingers in a flutter of modesty, but continued to smile. Others round the table laughed politely, but I could see that Lou was not joking.

"Li is too modest," Lou continued, making the old lady lower her eyes and shake her head in gentle denial. "She is creating some of the greatest hotel landscapes in the world in Shanghai and Bejing. They are like recreations of the Hanging Gardens of Babylon."

"Those gardens in Babylon," Li said, happy to take the opportunity to turn the spotlight away from herself. "They were built by a Syrian king to please one of his concubines; they say she was Persian and longed for the landscape of her homeland. She asked the king to imitate them through the artifice of a planted garden."

"Gardening is in Li's blood," Lou explained, making her lower her eyes again. "Her father created many of the greatest gardens of China before the revolution destroyed so much."

"We have been able to save many of them," Li said, "even after so long. Gardens are more resilient to the forces of barbarism than buildings."

28

The new leader rode into the palace like a conquering hero, his image repeating a hundred million times on news screens around the world with the dust churning up from beneath the wheels of the speeding jeep and his white robes flowing in the wind. His hair was wild and he had a surprisingly thick black growth on his chin considering it had only been a few days since I had seen him clean shaven and carefully groomed over lunch in Belgravia. In fact these few simple changes of image meant that I didn't recognize him as I first listened with the rest of the world to his declaration of victory over tyranny, as if overthrowing Mo had been all his own work. I did feel he seemed vaguely familiar but assumed I had seen him around the palace somewhere during the many hours that I had spent wandering aimlessly, killing time. I was only half watching the television which was my constant companion in the house as I endlessly tidied in preparation for each visit from prospective buyers, when Lou's phone call that brought the pieces together.

"Have you seen him on the news?" were Lou's opening words.

"The new President? Yes. He looks like George Clooney riding in to save the world."

"He was always the cleverest at manipulating media images," Lou went on. "We should have guessed what he was planning."

"Oh, it's the Minister!" I blurted, unable to control my shock at not having realized. "He's been planning this all along?"

"You didn't recognize him?" Lou laughed. "I think his rise is more opportunistic than planned. Nature abhors an empty space. If you uproot a tree and leave the earth bare weeds will soon spread across the gap, covering the wound until a new tree can take root."

"Is his arrival a problem for your gardening plans?"

"He is making out that it is all his doing but it will make no difference to the Chinese or the Indians, they will be happy to do business with whoever is in power. You need to be patient in times like this, give the soil time to heal and for the new growth to take root."

At the end of the phone call I went online to try to find more about what the minister was saying. It didn't take many clicks of the mouse before I found what I was looking for. It seemed that the Minister had been serious when he boasted that he was going to start writing again. I wondered if there was another ghostwriter beavering away in the background on a different brief to the one I was given, or was the Minister actually this fluent with his pen?

"This is our opportunity to put an end to the corruption that has sucked the lifeblood from our beloved country, taking the money that should have been invested in an infrastructure to support all the people and providing wealth for a few greedy people at the top. There are bank accounts in Switzerland that are bulging with the revenues of our oil fields, filled with the sweat of hard working men and women who are denied the schools they deserve for their children and the hospitals they need when they grow sick from labouring under the yoke. The fields that once supported us grew barren and the shops grew empty, while they feasted at the palace and flew in their private jets. They have sold our birthright to the Chinese, not just the future rights to our precious oil but the beloved land beneath our feet as well. But now it is time for them to repay us. They have the chemicals that will make our soil rich and the markets that will buy our produce, but they must be made to ensure that we are paid fairly for our labours and that every one of our citizens has a full belly and a tree to sit beneath in the midday heat."

I pictured Li and Khan sitting round the table in Italy, both so deferential to Lou, and the Minister in his previous sleek persona lunching in Belgravia with the lawyer and Zana who apparently held the purse strings and new patterns began to form in my mind.

29

"I'm flying over to London tomorrow."

The modest picture quality that Skype offers can often add a slight otherworldliness to the image of those you are talking to and at that moment Caroline seemed more beautiful than I could ever remember her looking. Maybe that was also partly because her words caused my eyes to mist over, adding to the unreal, soft focus, disconnected feel of the whole conversation. I couldn't completely trust that my mind was not playing tricks on me. For a few seconds it was like the intervening year had never happened, like I was speaking to the girl I had first met all those years ago.

"That's great," I said, unable to think of any words that could possibly convey even a portion of the wave of joy that was flooding through my body at that moment.

"Yes," she smiled and lowered her eyes. She was probably looking at something else on her screen while talking, but that tiny gesture of the eyelids made her seem flirtatious and shy in a way that forced my heart to lurch in my chest. "Yes, it is. Listen, there's somebody I want you to meet."

"Okay." I didn't even bother to ask who that might be. I didn't care. Caroline was coming back to me. The old Caroline. I was going to be given a chance to start again. In fact I'm not sure that her words lodged in my brain at all, because I didn't give any more thought to who this person that she wanted me to meet might be as I made frantic preparations to bring her home from the airport.

I didn't know if she was going to want to come back to the house or whether she wanted to cut the whole place out of her mind, but I spent the afternoon tidying away every scrap of evidence in the garden that might remind her that there had once been a tree house. I dismantled the last of the animal pens as well, piling everything onto one gigantic bonfire and feeling a huge wave of elation as the flames licked up into the sky, like they were cleansing the whole garden of the horror it had witnessed. By the time I had finished mowing the lawn it was dark and there was nothing but a glowing pile of embers to show what I had been doing with the previous hours. Had the physical exertion not left me so exhausted, I probably would not have been able to sleep that night because of the constant pounding of my heart in my ears. I was still too excited to eat breakfast the following morning before heading straight to the airport, many hours too early for her expected flight.

The caffeine that I then used to fill the waiting hours did nothing to calm my palpitations. It was how I imagine performers must feel as they prepare to step out in front of an important audience. I tried reading a newspaper to make the time move faster, but nothing held my attention apart from the deadly-slow movements of the flight arrivals board which stretched above the doors that I couldn't stop staring at. I have no memory of the moments immediately after she walked through those doors, pushing her luggage on a trolley, apart from the hug. We can't have clung to one another for more than a minute, but it felt like forever and I don't think I would ever have been able to bring myself to release her if she hadn't wriggled free and started telling me what we were going to be doing next.

"We're getting a train up to Birmingham this afternoon," she said, "so we have to get home and sort ourselves out. I've told Ali we'll meet him this evening."

She barely glanced at the garden when we got home, concentrating on repacking a smaller suitcase while I booked us a hotel room close to Birmingham New Street Station.

"Ali was a poet who we published at Petteridge," she had explained in the car. "He fell foul of your friend by writing articles critical of the regime." I let that one pass. "Arnold kept more in touch with him than I did, but I would hear about him occasionally from other writers in the country. He disappeared a couple of years ago. No one was sure what happened. There was a bit of a fuss and PEN took up his case for a while, but no one was able to track down where he might be imprisoned so there was a limit to what they could do. Most people thought he had been killed and his body had been spirited away. Now he's surfaced and he wants to write a book about his experiences and about his country. He was one of the prisoners under the palace gardens."

"If he's a writer, why does he need me?"

"He was a writer, and maybe he will be again, but there's an urgency about this book because of the change of regime and he is not in any fit state to sit down and write a book after what he has been through. Anyway, poetry is very different."

"How did he find you, now that Petteridge is closed down?"

"I've stayed in touch with a lot of people from those days. The Internet has made so much possible."

I thought of the hours and hours I had watched her as she sat beside Becky's bed, tapping away at her screen as she waited for the moment of miraculous recovery that never came. To my shame I had never asked her what she was doing or who she was talking to. I was too wrapped up in my own misery to be able to reach out even that little bit. Perhaps if I had, we would have been able to communicate more during those long, terrible days and nights. But we were communicating now and I didn't want to dwell on the many things that I could and should have done differently in the past. I was being given another chance, a "new growing season" as Lou might have said, and I didn't intend to waste it by brooding on the long, cold, hard emotional winter that had led up to it.

The train to Birmingham was crowded so it wasn't possible for us to talk openly, but Caroline showed me a number of articles on her laptop. To start with I couldn't concentrate, constantly wanting to stare at her, but she kept sending me back to the screen like a patient teacher with a promising but slightly reluctant pupil, until the things I was reading finally caught my attention and I began to pay proper attention. By the time we were in the hotel room I had taken in the full horror of what had been going on in those terrible cells we had fled past with Mo in his failed bid to escape his fate.

"How did Ali manage to get away?" I wanted to know in between Caroline's calls to a succession of mobile numbers as she tried to track down the address we were going to be meeting at.

"That's the story you need to get from him," she said. "That will provide the narrative drive over which he can talk about the politics and the background in the whole region. He has been an active dissident for years, but it will be the escape which will catch the attention of readers. That's why he is going to need your help with the structure."

I was now as fully hooked on the story as she was, but I still couldn't stop myself from staring at her. She looked so well compared to the last time I had seen her. Her mother must have managed to feed her up a bit, I decided, with all that home cooking. She actually looked happy, something I had never thought I would see again.

"Okay," she said as she hung up from yet another call. "We have an address. Are you ready?"

"Completely."

The taxi took us to a street that couldn't have been more anonymous, just another turning off a busy high road, lined with scruffy lines of terraced of houses and parked cars. The front garden of the number we had been given was filled with bins and there was more rubbish discarded around them. A buddleia which had started as a mere weed pushing through the paving stones had grown into a straggly tree, its leaves greyed with city dust. There were blankets pinned to the windows but it was still possible to see that the lights were on. We tried the bell but could hear no sound inside the door. We knocked but there was still no response. Caroline started phoning again and eventually got through to someone and a few minutes later the door opened a crack and an old woman peered out at us.

"We've come to see Ali," Caroline said, but the old woman seemed not to hear, just staring and sucking on her teeth until a young man in a grubby t-shirt and track suit bottoms appeared above her and gently steered her away.

He opened the door wide enough to stick his head out and look behind us to ensure there was no one else and then stood back to let us in. As we were taken through to the kitchen at the back of the house I glanced through an open door into the sitting room. There were people of every age sitting on every surface, staring back at me. A television flickered soundlessly in the corner. There was more talk in the kitchen where a young woman was boiling a kettle to make tea and some men were sitting round a table covered in open takeaway boxes.

"We've come to see Ali," Caroline said again and an emaciated looking man nodded his acceptance of this fact. "Ali?"

He didn't stand up but pressed the palms of his hands together and lowered his head in a modest greeting. I noticed that he had no fingernails and was missing the little fingers of both hands.

"I'm Caroline," she said, "this is my husband, the writer I was telling you about. It is such an honour for us to meet you at last. I am a huge fan of your writing."

"Thank you," was all he said.

"What if you can't find a publisher willing to take it on?" I asked her later, once we were back in the hotel room.

"I think we should publish it ourselves," she said. "God knows we've had enough experience between us over the years. And you've got your ill-gotten gains from the regime which we can use."

"True," I said, feeling ridiculously pleased when she laughed.

"Listen," she said, sitting down on the bed beside me and taking my hand. "There's someone else I want you to meet."

She gently opened my fingers and pressed my palm against her belly. I think at that moment I stopped breathing for a while, hardly daring to think what she was telling me.

"You remember that day at the clinic, in the room overlooking LA?"

"Of course," I replied.

"Everything is mended by the soil," Lou had said. "Floating like pollen in search of more fertile soil."